UNBINDING

ISAAC

A Novel

ABBY I. MILLER

For Jacob Aladar and Margot Andora. To the moon and back, with every iota of my being.

PROLOGUE

15 Heshvan, 5699
November 9, 1938

Isaac feels the sound of his brother's breathing guide him closer to sleep. He listens closely, trying to follow his parents' movements on the floor beneath him. In his mind, he watched his mother putting away dishes, following the sound of her feet across the kitchen, the clacking of plate on plate, and the opening and closing of drawers. He pictured his father, quiet, reading in the corner. But now the wind outside has drowned them out, pressing insistently against the frosted window beside his bed, trying to get inside.

Squeezing his eyes shut, he shimmies further from the wall and tucks the ends of his blanket beneath him on all sides. The weather calms, and Isaac can catch the sound of his parents climbing the stairs and moving past his bedroom. Finally silent, finally warm, he drifts to sleep.

At that moment, someone, somewhere not so far away, breaks a window and strikes a match.

זָכוֹר

Syllables and prefixes. Words as plants and children, a gene-
alogy of sound. The root of "to record" is in the heart, as in
to remember by heart. The root of "to mourn" is either to
remember or else to die—to wither away.

בְּכוֹר

THE ELDEST SON

I love winter in this city. The endless grey. It's like a wool cloak that muffles everything." Seda traced a tic-tac-toe board into the fog her breath had made on the passenger window. She was right; there was little sound except the push-and-crunch of the snow tires carving into the slush and the hesitant squeaking of her finger's touch on the glass. Jake listened and nodded. She was right; the air was thick in winter, moisture softening the beat of her words.

"Dull and quiet," he said, flipping on the rear defrost. "Although, it could just be the neighbourhood."

Seda shifted in her seat, pushing her back against the door and looking at her boyfriend. "No, it's the city. Everything is all slow and soft. See even now." She raised her hand to gesture to the snowbanks that lined the residential street they were creeping down. "You could hit the gas, spin the tires, and still the most that would happen is we'd go shooting out and land quietly into one of those. Our impact would be noiseless, it would be nothing." On both sides of the car, the snowbanks rested like sinister pillows: blindingly white and rounded on their tops, and then stained black by car exhaust and jagged as they stretched towards the street, caught in-between being snow and being ice.

She's right, Jake thought, even if we crashed, even if we died right here and now, not even that would make a sound. He decided it was comforting, that thought...the impactlessness.

"Like airbags made of ice." Seda talked to herself more than to Jake. He'd been extra quiet, but who could blame him; he'd had a rough couple of weeks. Seda smiled and he caught it with the corner of his eye.

"How about you drop me off, then go and get us some food?" Jake's voice was light, forced into something almost upbeat. "I'm not really in the mood to finish off leftovers and there's nothing else at the house." He reached out to put his hand on her thigh.

"Okay. I can do that."

Jake squeezed her leg and pulled his hand back to the wheel. They made their way up the rest of the street in silence, Seda fiddling with the heat controls and passenger side vents. Near the end of the cul-de-sac, Jake pulled into his father's driveway.

It was the only house on the block with snow on the driveway. At every other house, the shovelers had been out and busy. Jake's father had always had an Italian man who used to do the shovelling: shovelling in winter and planting in summer. It had never occurred to Jake that they might cancel their services. The man, once young and alone, now older and with a boy who looked just like him when Jake had been little — thick eyebrows and a long face, a smiling hello that disappeared as soon as it was shared — had always just come. Jake would have to call a service to come in and do it so that things could be moved out of the house more easily. If not, it would be a subject for chit-chat in the neighbourhood, even with a death in the house to preoccupy the gossips. And for some reason, though he certainly did not know what, the thought of that bothered him. Arrangements — more arrangements— would have to be made.

Jake undid his seat belt but left the car turned on. He turned to Seda. "Just pick up something easy for tonight. It's not worth getting groceries."

"You go inside. I'll figure something out and be right back."

Jake got out of the car and held the driver's door open. Seda slipped behind the wheel and pulled the door shut behind her. The tires rolled noiselessly back down the driveway and into the street. Left alone, with no options and no company, Jake entered his father's house.

Jake took off his shoes, shoving them into the corner by the door, and let his coat fall on the dark wood banister that led upstairs. He moved slowly but directly into the basement.

Even though it was the most cluttered, the basement was the cleanest area in the house. It had been ever since Jake's mom died. All the light bulbs were new; even when Ike got sick, he made sure to change them every few weeks. Jake had argued with him on the phone about it. He told his father it was ridiculous for a man in his condition to be going up and down ladders. Ike argued back that changing the bulbs wasn't bad for him, "but to read in dim light makes you go blind and then you can't read at all. That would be worse." Jake never offered to come over and fix the lights for him, and Ike never asked.

A low desk sat in the middle of the room; it was the desk from Jake's room when he was little. There had been a folding table there before, the kind other people in other houses used to play cards. The area under the desk was taken up with white cardboard banker's boxes, heavy with paper and clippings. These should have been scattered throughout the room, their lids half off and their insides fanned out or piled high on every available surface. They would have been except that the last time Jake and Seda came to visit, she thought it might be nice to help neaten the house and tidy things up, so she stuffed the paper innards back inside their paper bodies and stacked them where they couldn't be tripped over. It was a good thing Ike had been too sick to make it downstairs, or he would have been furious at her for touching his private things. Ike was a private man, as many old men and many collectors are.

The walls of the basement were lined with filing cabinets of various sizes and colours: the wide green ones had always been there, ever since Jake could remember; the thinner beige ones, already rusty down the sides, were only a few years old and presents from Jake who found them at a garage sale; the rest of them, mismatched dwarfs and dented tin giants, were leftovers from the back of Ike's store. Each cabinet sat looking out of place like a stranger at a party full of strangers. The only uniformity was that each was now topped with a thick pad of light grey dust as though strangers at a party all wearing the same bad toupee.

Ike had been a voracious reader. But he wasn't one of those types of people who read the news only to have something to discuss at cocktail parties and on the train, indulging in convenient small talk to make them look worldly and aware. Ike never chatted about current events, at least not that Jake ever heard, and he was no snob over what he was reading — one paper was as good as the next, which made a lot of sense if, like Ike, you read at least four papers a day. Even when Jake was little and money was tight, there was always enough to fund his father's reading. His mother, Rose, who never learned to read English, romanticized her husband's collection. She called him a lover of words. Of course, when she said it, the compliment dripped heavy with her accent; "word" always sounded like "*wort,*" the pronunciation never quite escaping her Yiddish.

Jake knew that insurance documents and bank statements would all be down here, as compulsively kept as the newspaper clippings and old letters thrown in together, no reason or system beyond one of Ike's own devising known only to him. And while Ike had never asked him, Jake knew that he had to go through and sort everything properly down here. The rest of the house didn't matter, but anyone else looking for or through his collection would have made Ike uncomfortable. Exposed. Even scared. Even with him gone, this was the place Jake knew he had to be. It was the one task he had to take on for himself to wrap up his father's life and clear it out where no one would see it. He wouldn't be tidying up loose ends for his father—Ike wouldn't have had those—but it was tidying up his father himself. As different as they were, something deep inside Jake understood, as he himself would have felt the same way.

He walked over to the first filing cabinet near the bottom of the stairs. It was as good a place as any to start, so he pulled on the handle of the top drawer, and with the shrill cry of metal against metal, the drawer gave way. The entire filing cabinet moved with it, shaking the top layer of dust onto his sleeve. Jake went on to try the second drawer, but it wouldn't budge.

He fingered the small silver keyhole under the handle. "Locked." He tried the bottom drawer, pulling harder than necessary. The olive-green metal responded smoothly, startling Jake; the drawer slid out too quickly and more dust released itself into the air.

Jake moved from drawer to drawer, cabinet to cabinet; some drawers were locked while others slid easily open. He left these slightly ajar and moved over to the collection of boxes and folders. *Fucking random*, he thought, *makes no sense at all.* "What kind of person locks drawers in their own basement?" Jake asked the empty room. But of course, he knew. And "locked," he thought, not "locks."

Sitting at the desk, Jake looked inside its single drawer. The lip of the drawer was still covered with ink, his ink, from time spent drawing when he should have been doing homework, his words and letters carved into the soft wood. In the little tray that sat waiting for pencils and erasers, he found a clump of small keys, tangled together on a fat rubber band. He knew without trying that these would open the locked drawers. An unexpected wave of relief slid over his shoulders; the drawers were locked because they could be. Simple as that.

Jake pulled one of the heavy boxes out from underneath the desk. With a low grunt, he picked it up and dropped it onto the wooden desktop. He decided to start sorting through these, the most recent of his father's clippings, and then work on the filing cabinets. Jake knew what he was expecting—everything piled together; newspaper trimmings would be stacked together with pages pulled from magazines, various organizations' newsletters folded beside correspondence from friends, were his father to have had any.

Jake reached both arms into the box and pulled out a pile of newspaper clippings. He fanned these out on the desk in front of him the way his father used to do. Some familiar titles caught his eye from the same papers his father had always read: *Canadian Jewish Chronicle, Jewish Free Press, The Gazette.* Jake knew that in the other boxes, in the other drawers, he would see more of the same, including his father's favourites: *Der Kanader Odler, Canadian Jewish Review, The Jewish Times, Alliance-Francoise,* and the free papers distributed on the metro.

Other people, everyone else, would read the metro papers on their way to or from some place or another and then leave them behind the way one was supposed to. Ike would pick these papers up from the seats on the train or the aisles of the bus and take them home with him. The free metro papers used to publish bits of poetry that Ike would translate and then read aloud to his wife. Rose loved it, though the words never sounded quite as pretty in Yiddish. To Jake, the translations always sounded rough, like the words had once been whole pieces but when they came out of his father's mouth, they were somehow broken, jagged. Ike would read the poems and Rose would listen, then he would disappear into the basement with the papers, and she would just go on with her day.

Rose and Jake never followed Ike and never went into the basement alone. It wasn't a rule; it was just the way it was. When Jake was eleven and his mother died, very little in the house changed, or at least very little that could be seen. And the way it had been was the way it continued to be. Jake didn't know until now that the drawers were locked because he'd never tried to open them in over 30 years. Now, with his father gone, it still wasn't any real curiosity that sent him down there. It was rather a desire to clear things out and get the house on the market.

———

Seda descended the basement stairs, stopping halfway and leaning over the railing to find Jake sitting on the floor in front of the desk, dug into a trench of papers, garbage bags, and boxes.

"Holy," Seda whistled, Jake raising his head. "At least it looks like you've been making some progress."

Jake had forgotten that she was in the house. Other than

her voice calling down to him, letting him know she was back with food (and that must have been hours ago) , he had spent the entire day mired in the basement. It occurred to him then how easy it must have been for his father to lose track of time—of everything—down here in the midst of all this.

"Sorry. I didn't really expect to get this into it, and I'm maybe only a quarter of the way through it all." Jake stretched his arms out in front of him and grabbed the desk leg, pulling himself up.

"S'no problem. Lots to do up here. I threw everything from the fridge and pantry out except for what we'll need for dinner and snack stuff while we're here."

Jake nodded; he was wading through the mess, bending himself around the opened garbage bags and folded cardboard. "What time is it? There's no clock."

"And no window either. It's dark. A little after six. Zalman should be here soon."

Jake reached the bottom of the staircase and climbed towards her. He paused one step away and kissed her softly on the shoulder. Seda felt the familiar press of his lips through her cotton turtleneck. He was exhausted. With his hand on the small of her back, Jake led her out of the stairwell, turning off the lights behind him.

Seda had bought paper plates and plastic cutlery which she used to set the dining room table, having spent the day cleaning and dusting Ike's dishes so they could be properly packed. Jake planned on selling them, so they had to be in good condition. "I found your mom's china, I'm guessing."

Seda examined the bent prong of a two-cent fork, not seeing the look on Jake's face. She placed the fork down and turned to him. "Navy with gold, like around the rim." Seda traced a small vine in the air with her fingers. "It was all packed up in these padded plastic holders that zip shut. In the bottom of the cabinet."

"Yeah, that's hers."

"I put it near the front door. I figured it was something you'd want to keep."

Jake joined her at the dining room table, a wad of cheap paper napkins in his hand, the kind his mother hated, with picnic designs printed on the flimsy tissue. "Thanks."

"Where did your mom get china?"

"I don't know. Wedding present maybe...the normal way."

"I know, I just..." Seda pulled out a chair and dropped herself down, "It looks expensive, Jake. And I just thought maybe it was a family heirloom."

Jake sighed. He knew what was coming, as they'd had this talk before. "Maybe you should be keeping more, looking more closely," she added.

"Listen to me," Jake cupped her cheeks in his hands. They were shaped like upside-down hearts. "She had nothing. He had nothing. I know you're trying, but it's not the same for me."

"Like it would be for me."

"Like it would be for you. There's not..." Jake searched for his words, releasing her face; the heat from his hands having

10

warmed her blush into an apple fire. "I just know what I want to keep. What there is that's worth taking."

The front door opened, and heavy footsteps shuffled in, quickly shutting out the chill of the street behind them. Zalman coughed in that old man, old Europe way: a sound like wet sandpaper rendered more to signal his presence than to clear out his throat. Seda rubbed Jake's arm and went to the front door to greet their guest while he finished setting the table.

––––––––––

The entire meal was spent with Zalman asking Seda questions about everything: her childhood, her family, her work, her friends. He seemed to want to know everything about her and was gushingly pleased with every detail she offered up. Seda would reciprocate, and the old man would weave a short, charming anecdote in response, talking about his wife, his dogs, the travel over before deftly swinging the focus back in her direction. Jake sat there just watching them, already so comfortable and at ease with each other. Their only real connection was through him, but already they didn't need him there. They lit each other up and in turn, lit up the room. The whole house seemed warmer, fuller, than it had been in years. Jake wondered if the rooms themselves remembered as he did what life was like before his mother died. When most days, when she was having good days at least, her voice was always somewhere to be heard. Rose liked to talk... and to hum. She was always humming to herself when she was alone, filling the spaces around her. His mother's humming had been the background soundtrack of his childhood, except on those other days. The bad ones. Then the house was perfectly silent and still, the way it had stayed after she was gone.

———————

"She's a kind girl, offered me a ride to my plane." Seda had taken the paper plates into the kitchen, the Styrofoam containers and balled-up napkins precariously balanced, swaying with her compact frame as it moved out of the dining room. She had made an effort to clear everything in one trip, and now, having left the two men alone, she switched on the radio in the kitchen. Jake knew what she was doing, giving him and Zalman their space and a chance to talk before the old man left Montreal the next day.

Zalman filled his chair with layers of cloth and folds of tan skin. He had only ever been to Canada once before, and not in winter. Now he found himself feeling constantly cold. He had spent the past week bundled in the entire contents of his suitcase. Tonight, he wore a navy collared shirt under a maroon vest and a beige cardigan. He wore his scarf around his neck, the way he had for the length of his trip, taking it off only briefly during Ike's funeral before putting it back on, wrapping it tightly up and around his chin at the cemetery. He sat sucking his teeth with his tongue, a habit Jake had heard many times over the phone when Zalman called for his father but insisted on talking to Jake for a while before the phone could be handed over. Sometimes the old man even

12

insisted to Ike that Jake be put back on, being so eager to know what he had done that day and how were his friends and school. Jake was forced to endure the long-distance sucking noise for several minutes over the phone after his mother had died; Zalman had wanted to say something to the poor boy, his cumbersome English punctuated by sad pauses and the smack of his tongue as it fell off his bicuspids.

"She's had a rough week." Jake sighed in the direction of the kitchen. "She's been trying so hard."

"We've all had a rough week." Zalman rested one hand in the centre of his wide chest. "She must have liked your father a lot."

Jake shrugged and looked at this man he had met in person for only the second time nine days ago with an accent similar enough to his father's that every word out of his mouth made Jake wince. A man his mother had once told him to call "uncle." "She cared about him a lot actually, not that it mattered."

Zalman tapped his yellowed index finger softly against his chest and looked at Jake through one eye.

"Almost everyone who bothered to show up to the shivah were her friends, her family, coming to be polite."

Zalman nodded in rhythm. "Her people would know how to mourn."

Seda's friends and family had not known exactly what to bring to a shivah, as it was a foreign concept to almost all of them. Seda told them that it was the visitor's role to bring food for the mourning family, so they had one less thing to worry about—a cultural detail Jake had remembered vaguely from his mother's passing when the house was filled with home-made platters brought over by her friends. He was unable to recall, however, what the food had been, merely describing it to Seda as depressing. "It's supposed to be depressing. Everything is. We eat but we're not happy about it."

His best friend Leah had suggested they order a couple platters from a local deli or restaurant that would know what was appropriate. And so they had all done that, going to the same one restaurant that had been suggested. While Jake and Zalman sat in the low, hard chairs provided by the funeral home, Seda's parents and friends hovered in the kitchen, trying to rearrange plates and shift morsels so that some of the dishes looked different. For seven days, the house had been filled with matching platters of blintzes, bagels, lox, bowls of egg salad, rugellah. It was a scene he overheard Leah describe as "death sponsored by deli."

Throughout the shivah, the two men had been pretty much left on their own in the living room. The morning of the funeral, the rabbi asked how many would be sitting for the deceased. Before Jake could answer, Zalman offered a number. "Two." Jake resisted, telling him that it was appreciated, the thought and all, but not necessary. Zalman closed his eyes then and with one hand on Jake's shoulder, leaned in close. "Please, no. No." He shook his head, "I didn't get to sit for my brothers. Please now, let me do this for Izzy. My friend. I would be honoured."

It had been awkward at first, silently sitting together that first morning, only a drizzle of guests passing in and out of the room, their coats and hats already ushered into the den by Leah and her mother. Almost all of them were strangers, even the old Jews who had genuinely come for his father and not as Seda's guests. Most of them had been friends of Rose, in their early seventies. They offered their condolences not with words but with grandmotherly gestures, grasping Jake's one hand in both of theirs and holding it tightly, shaking firmly. They all had sad eyes, damp as if they were about to cry, but Jake knew these women who were just like his mother, knew better. They had finished their actual crying years ago, but mourning was a way of life.

No one had said anything about the strange old man sitting beside Jake; no one knew Ike or his son well enough to have been curious. Zalman was not a blood relative but the only type of family his father had ever spoken of.

"He could barely even bring himself to be nice to her. Couldn't deal with the idea of my Armenian girlfriend. How was I supposed to explain that to her? In three years, he could hardly bother to be civil."

The truth was, and Jake would never admit it, it had never seemed to bother Seda. As if she long ago accepted his indifference, just as she had accepted the reality of other older men and women's curt reactions and othering stares. Ike's coldness faded into the background of a simmering hostility she had not only grown used to in the city but had grown to expect.

Zalman shook his head, "You weren't listening to him. I know. He didn't not like her; she scared him."

Jake opened his eyes and mouth wide, his voice lilted by sarcasm. "Oh, well then. That's much better. Ridiculous, but much better."

Zalman laughed, "Not better, that is fair. But different?" He lifted his hand and let it drop three times on his chest, the thump of its landing absorbed in cotton padding. "You maybe never understand that. Things about your father you never saw quite right."

Jake lowered his head and shrugged, "More of his secrets, I guess."

"Secrets? Hah. No. Something is only a secret if someone asks you and you decide not to tell."

"Well, it's too late now." The thought was not new to Jake; it had been sitting in his belly since Ike's death, rumbling there at the strangest of times, never letting Jake forget its presence.

Zalman shrugged and spoke slowly, "Maybe." The two men sat together a moment, the quiet of the room scored by the music from the kitchen radio. Jake stared at his guest's feet; he had lent Zalman his father's house slippers. Jake decided he would ask his "uncle" to keep them. "Well, I like her a lot." Zalman sat forward in his seat and chuckled softly. "She says my name right." He raised his plastic cup to his lips, inhaling the last of the shallow pool of red wine. "We have time, some time. I can tell you what I know. All of it is yours anyway." He emphasized his offer by firmly smacking his chest with both hands, reaching them out towards Jake, empty but willing across the table. "What do you want to know?"

Jake had no questions ready. He thought for a moment again about the shivah, how different it had felt from what he remembered of his mother's. But of course, he had been a child when her heart gave out, and a child losing a parent is a tragedy. He was now a grown man. Being a grown man and losing a parent that—he could hear it in his father's voice—was life.

"Another time Zalman, thank you, really. But it's getting late, and this is your last night here."

"Another time. I promise."

———

A strong wind made its presence known against the front door, pressing hard against the house. Zalman took care to press his earlobes in under his hat before hugging Seda goodbye. The hug was long, warm, and real. She really liked him, in so short a time growing so fond. And he her, although, Jake thought, maybe he's just affectionate...just like that. It's not a detail his father would have mentioned or would have noticed in the first place. But Zalman looked like he meant the hug as a real embrace. He took Jake into his arms next. The old man's skin smelled of years of having been baked in the sun, something in its texture coming through even in the Montreal winter.

"Call me, anytime. Our difference is only a few hours, and I stay up late." Zalman rested both his hands on Jake's shouldders, squeezing him as tightly as he could with arthritic fingers. "Okay," Jake said, unable to meet Zalman's eyes, "I will. We will."

"Okay." Zalman winked at the younger man and reached for the door.

———————

The time it takes to pack up a life lies in the size of the life in question: how was it lived? And how widespread and scattered are the pieces of its impact? In Ike Langley's case, it was a contained life, nearly half of 86 years nestled within the four walls of a single home. By the third day of packing and sorting, Jake and Seda had gone through most of the house, putting everything in boxes, some marked for keeping, most to be sold. Jake spent almost all of his time in his father's basement, tangled up in Ike's papers—his collection. Seda came down occasionally with questions: did he want to keep the books? His mother's clothes? By the end of the second day, Jake had felt the need to flee the basement, as the room had become claustrophobic and unbearably lonely. But he was almost done then, so he had returned the next morning and slipped easily back into the pool of clippings, newspapers, and business receipts.

Jake pulled open the bottom drawer of a beige filing cabinet, its metal seams outlined in rust. Unlike the stuffed drawers and boxes he had been through, this drawer was nearly empty. Reaching in, Jake drew the meager contents into his arm and brought them to the desk. He laid his arm flat against the desktop, scanning the contents as they slid off his forearm and onto the wood. Before him sat an unmarked manila folder, wrapped in a wide brown elastic band, and a large brown envelope. The folder's rough edges had been rubbed soft by the pads of Ike's fingers, the corners curled outwards. The seam which held the two sides together had been meticulously scotch-taped several times over many years. The envelope appeared empty in comparison, flat and thin, only the slightest outline of its contents pressing out against the brown paper.

He decided to open the envelope first. There had been other envelopes, both legal and letter, some stuffed with receipts, others with a business statement or rough note jotted on paper. Jake's hand entered the envelope's mouth, searching. The tips of his fingers found something soft surrounded by loose threads. Letting the now empty envelope drop to the desk, Jake examined what he had found: the binding and jacket of a book, its body absent. He pressed the old brown leather jacket flat in his hand; the binding at its edges was still tight in some places, black thread coming loose in others. The inside of the front flap had been written on, the ink carved hard into the skin. Jake had to turn the book around so that the letters were not upside down. Laid open, the front cover was on the right-hand side. Under the bright light he could make the inscription out as Hebrew letters and Hebrew words. Jake recognized the twisted alphabet though he had long forgotten their sound. That didn't matter; he knew immediately what it said.

His father had always kept journals. Jake had found one

once when he was little and gone through it; it hadn't looked like a normal diary and besides, it wasn't written in English. Ike had caught his son trying to put the book back in the bedside table where he had found it. Instead of getting angry, Ike was silent. Jake asked his father why he didn't write in English and rather than answer, Ike had simply turned around and left the room.

The inside cover of that journal had been inscribed the same way with his father's name written in Hebrew letters. But the handwriting wasn't his father's. Even in another language, it was softer and rounder. The leather flap in his hands now was old, smooth, all the stitch work having been done by hand. Running his hands along the seams, Jake could feel something embossed on the outside of the jacket. Turning it over, he found the figure of a small horse pressed into the bottom left side of the front flap. So many boxes and filing cabinets. He hadn't even thought about the journals and why they hadn't been kept and filed away with everything else. Popping open box lids and scanning drawers, Jake looked for another journal, another piece of his father that could instantly be so real to him. But there was nothing. More clippings, more bank statements, more poetry. His father's other journals were nowhere to be found.

Jake returned to the desk, laid the soft leather gently in front of him, and moved his attention to the folder.

With one finger, he slid off the fat elastic and flipped the folder open, exposing its insides. The folder itself, now open in front of him, caught his eye. The front flap was covered in different colours of ink, his father's handwriting - a list, the contents of which stretched out in uneven lines across the width of the folder. Jake scanned the page searching for order, but there was none. Names of people sat squeezed in above names of places, dates bloomed in the crack between letters and many of the items were crossed out with a scribbled 'X' and a date beside them. None of the names were familiar, though he could tell they were Jewish. And Polish. Like his father's name had been before shedding its European layers at the Canadian border. Names that ended in "sky," "berg," "men," "off," and "vitch."

Other names, those of places, were even less familiar: Augustow, Krynki, Tykocin. Some place names were more familiar with titles of warm or distant destinations. There were Canadian cities, appropriated Native words and misguided British nostalgia which sat looking out of place on the page. He began thumbing through the items in the folder, matching names scribbled on pages, notes and envelopes with names in the list. An oversized paper clip held together a clump of obituaries with some of the highlighted names corresponding with lines on the folder.

Jake traced the letters with his pinkie finger. Every time his finger found a Canadian city, he circled the name beside it, searching his memory. If his father had known this person, if they had lived nearby, why didn't Jake remember hearing about them? Meeting them? As a kid he had only ever been shown off to his mother's friends. He would be brought into the room while the women smiled and

21

patted his cheeks. His mother would list off her son's great many assets, most of which were embellished, and if Jake tried to interrupt or even sigh, fierce stares from the gallery quickly shut him up. But his father had never brought friends home. And other than business, the only person Ike ever spoke to on the phone was Zalman.

Zalman, Zalman, Jake thought and eagerly searched the page. He found what he was looking for just below the middle of the page: in his father's handwriting, *Zeama Weiss <u>Krynki</u> – ~~200 Rue Des Rosiers, Paris,~~ ~~Le Presbytere, Mondion,~~ 17 Rue Verlet Hanus, Casablanca, 01 Morocco 011 212 2 27 92 18.* There he was: the old man who had sat with Jake just days before, now a trail of ink on the page. A tide of pressure raised itself and crashed against the inside of Jake's forehead, just above his eyes. Like the man had said, it's just a few hours difference; Jake should feel free to call anytime.

Placing the leather journal cover carefully inside, Jake closed the folder and re-secured it with the brown elastic band. He climbed with it held tightly under his arm to the top of the basement stairs. Stopping, Jake put the folder down on the top stair below the crack of the closed door. He looked at it for a moment, sitting there. The claustrophobia of the day before and the weight of the air in the room returned. Jake opened the door, stepped over the top step into the hallway and shut the basement, with all of its contents, behind him. He would deal with it later. Soon, but later.

Rose had loved Ike very much. She knew him in the unspoken ways only a wife could. He didn't have to tell himself to her; she could read his mind from the way he walked through a room. And she wanted her son to know Ike, too. He was her favourite story to tell. For example, Rose told her son that his father had travelled a lot through Poland with his uncle before the war, before Ike escaped. She said she wished she could smell in the air what Ike had, know what he had known, how he had known to run so maybe she too could have run and taken some of her family with her. "But," she would say shrugging her shoulders, offering her empty palms to the kitchen ceiling, "*ale alpee leshitose.*" Each to their own path. And it was Ike's path, not hers, that took him away from his parents and through the shtetls surrounding Bialystok (with names like Augustow, Krynki, Tykocin) that led him out of Europe.

———————

Jake had done his best to explain to Seda what he thought he'd found. She had been in his father's bedroom, taping up another box. She sat cross-legged on the bare mattress and as Jake began to speak, she leaned backwards, resting on her elbows. She said nothing, just listened, occasionally punctuating his words with silent oh's she formed with her lips. And when he was finished, she closed her eyes, shook her head and breathed loose a single word: "Huh."

Jake sat down on the floor in front of the bed. "I don't know why but it felt strange looking at it. It was there with everything else but... I just—it feels private. It feels private, but I did it anyway. Is that ok?"

"I guess so. Everything down there is yours now."

"Yup." Jake pulled at the carpet with his fingers, filling his hand with tufts of frizzy beige nylon and then sprinkling them back onto the floor.

"What are you going to do with it?"

Jake shrugged and swept his mess under the box spring. Seda pushed off her forearms and crawled towards the edge of the bed towards him. Her dark brown hair dangled over the edge of the bed, and she leaned her body forward, pressing her forehead to his. "These people might have known your dad. This is a gift."

Jake closed his eyes and kissed her. His hands found the ends of her long hair and he rubbed the smooth strands between the pads of his fingers before letting them fall away. Seda shifted weight back onto her heels, her face slipping away from him, too. "It's a good thing you went down there with your eyes wide open."

Jake looked at her. Seda let her eyes move around the many packed boxes in the room. "Last chance to open any of them up."

Jake scratched the scar on his right elbow and rubbed his cheek with his fist. Pointing to his mother's side table, covered in chunks of mirror and coloured glass, "Only that. The rest can go but I want that."

Rose had spent her days, after losing her only son to day school, working in the back office and storage space at his father's store. She said it was because she preferred not to have to try and talk to customers but, in truth, it was for the light. She preferred the light back there. The showroom was bright, full of every size and shape of mirror, framed or carved, reflecting the overhead lights and the sunlight from the storefront, moving through the hanging and displayed glassware. The whole place glowed as light was constantly cast, reflected, and bent. Rose never liked it. It was too much. In the backroom with the broken merchandise, shards of glass everywhere that made the floor crunch like sand, she could see a beam of light directly... where it came from and where it was going.

One day she'd decided to take up a new hobby. She came home with a bucket full of broken mirror pieces and coloured glass. She spent the entire rest of the day, into the evening after his father had come home, carefully picking pieces of glass out of the white plastic and gluing them onto her nightstand. When it was mostly covered, she decided it was finished and not one other thing should be added—not even mortar.

Years later, Jake had been in the bedroom watching Rose sleep. He wanted to kiss her but was worried that he'd lose his balance and disturb her. It was another fitful sleep...the kind she would fall into after one of her episodes. So instead, he rested his elbows on the table and leaned over to get his head near hers on the pillow. His skin dug into the sharp-edged cracks, and when he left the room, he noticed little zig zags of blood moving quickly down his arms. Only the right side had scarred, stretched white X's hardly visible now in the folds of his skin.

———————

"I'm taking that side table and the rest can go. I think we should call it a day." Jake got up to leave the room. He stopped at the door frame and picked up one of the boxes to take downstairs. "Don't worry, Seda." He looked at her sitting on the bed, watching him, "My eyes are open."

———————

The folder sat on the desk in front of him. Jake had spent that morning picking through the contents. Some of what was there was obvious, even if the names and places rang no bells — an obituary for a woman named Bronya, a birth announcement with the last name Grunsweig, an address on a note, labelled only with the Hebrew letter *mem* — but most of the clippings and items were a mystery to Jake no matter how hard he searched the pages. He had given up and decided to work from the list. There were only seven names not crossed out that were matched up to nearby cities. He would start with those. At first, he planned on calling people on the phone, stating who he was and waiting for them to explain why they were in a folder in his father's basement. It didn't make sense that they would know, or know what Jake wanted to hear, but it was the only plan he had so far.

An hour on the phone with the Jewish Genealogical Society of Montreal had gotten him his first number. Jake had lied to the secretary, claiming himself a long-lost relative. "I just want to clarify, Mr. Langley, you're related to the Frankls how?" He told her it was through marriage somehow, some distant connection, but he could tell she wasn't buying it. His specifics were too vague; he thought they lived in Montreal for a time but couldn't say when. Then Jake mumbled something about the Holocaust, how everyone got mixed up, but they were from the same village. Jake kept talking but he could feel his words had already loosened the coil of suspicion on the other end of the line. Bingo, he thought, the magic word. She agreed to search for the information. "I don't see how it could hurt. I hope you find what you're looking for."

When he'd called the number, however, the woman who answered explained that her parents had long since moved to Florida and only she was left in Montreal now. They both agreed it was probably best not to try to bother them there.

For a moment, Jake stared at the folder. Then he picked up a scrap of paper, and using it a ruler, very carefully crossed out the Montreal address, writing "Florida" neatly in the margin beside it. The way his father would have done.

Jake heard Seda open the apartment door, and Leah's voice — which seemed always a little louder than even she expected it to be — asking how he was doing and if she could interrupt. There was a knock on the door to what served as his study, and Leah pushed her way into the room sideways, using her hip to force the handle. She had two white Styrofoam trays of take-out, one in each hand. "You guys have to eat. I brought

Seda a wrap but couldn't decide what you'd want more." She crossed the room and held out both trays over his desk.

"What's in them?" Jake took the food out of her hands and popped open the containers' lids.

"Chicken Caesar and garlic bread. Some kind of pasta and meat sauce."

Jake handed back the lighter container. "Pasta, thanks." Leah reached into her purse and pulled out a plastic bag with a single set of cutlery, a wetnap, and one tiny packet each of salt and pepper. "That's what I thought you'd say." She dropped the utensils on the desk and went back into her bag, producing a worn, coil-bound book. Placing it down on the desk, she shifted her weight to her left foot and used the toe of her right shoe to scratch her calf. "Thought this might be of help, too. And I assume you don't have one." The cover was two pieces of textured pink construction paper which sandwiched together a stack of white paper almost a Toonie thick. Jake pulled the *Jewish Community Phonebook 2007* over the table towards him. "It's a couple years old but the only one I have. You never know. My mom always refused to get one when I was younger. Still can't get her head wrapped around it. Everyone putting their names, and addresses even, together in a book voluntarily."

She turned and took a step towards the door before stopping and facing him again. "You know I could try to help you. Help more." She smiled and shook her head, "You know I love a project."

"I do know. I think I may be one of your projects."

28

"My favourite project since we were teenagers, though I'm not sure I'd call you one my successes just yet."

"Ouch," he feigned hurt. "A failure then?"

She took a moment to think about it before she replied. "Not a failure, just not yet finished. A work in progress."

Jake smiled.

Leah shrugged off the moment and rose on her heels to turn again and leave him to himself. Just before she did, however, she gave him the look he had gotten used to seeing in the past two weeks. It was somewhere in between a smile and a wince. He had received it from almost everyone, followed shortly by either, "I'm so sorry to hear that" or "Really, is there anything I can do?" It was a face he'd seen before and yet only really hurt him coming from her, who should have known better. But Jake knew it was a genetic twitch, a face passed down to her, the pained look which really said, "I'm sorry but I have nothing else to say."

———————

He listened for a few minutes to the two women talking in the kitchen, muffled voices, at first one concerned and the other reassuring, then quickly moving to the sound of two friends catching up. Letting his lunch congeal, Jake found the next local name on the list and flipped open the phonebook. He wasn't sure why, but he was actually surprised to see it there: the same surname and initial that his father had written down, no address but a number listed. It wasn't until after he dialled that he got nervous. He lost count of the rings—had there been too many? At what point is it rude not to let go, hang up and try again another time? A soft female voice interrupted his worrying. "Hello?"

"Hello? Hello. I'm looking for a, uh," Jake glanced down at where his finger sat on the page, "Mr. Yanofsky." Jake licked his lips and tried again to make out his father's slippery handwriting, a C and a P something. "P, maybe Peter?"

"I think you must be looking for my brother."

"Yes, maybe. I was hoping I could speak with him."

"But he's not at this number."

"Oh." Jake was playing with the phone cord, wrapping its fat coils around his index finger. "I see."

"I could give you his number. Let me get my book." Jake could hear the sound of the receiver being laid down against something hard on the other end. He began to search his desk for something to write on...a spare piece of paper. Sticking a pen in his mouth, he pulled the cap off and reached into his desk to grab his notepad.

The soft voice returned, "You're still there?"

Jake let the pen cap drop from between his lips. "I am. I'm here."

"Alright, here goes..."

כִּסְלֵו

KISLEV

§

Kislev 5699

December 1938

The tips of my fingers are alive...the only part of my right arm that is. It feels like thousands of electric ants crawling all over my skin. I try to shake my sleeping arm awake, but nothing seems to work; my one dead arm, the whole rest of me trying to shock it into life. I could slap it against my leg...that might work, but it would probably wake up the other passengers. Not my uncle though. He snores terribly. So does my brother but not like my uncle. It's the only way to tell that he's not dead —he sleeps so deep. He moves though, jostles and gets shoved around on the seat like the rest of us. He slid onto me last night and it didn't wake him. I didn't know if I would be able to breathe with all of his weight on my chest, but then we went around a corner and I was freed. One like-dead uncle, one like-dead arm. Between the cold and the rocking wagon, it's probably been asleep all night like him. I use my left hand to slip the right into the outer pocket of my coat. Let it wake up in a few hours when he does. I could jump all over him, and this wagon could hit every rock in the road, but only the sunrise wakes him. And even then, only enough to pray.

I hope we never have to travel through the night again. I may be too old to miss my family but not too old to miss my bed. Even if I have to share the room with snoring Ben, anything is better than this. Uncle said tomorrow night we'll stay in a house with the cantor's family. We might have to share a room but at least not a bed. And it is Shabbat, so after dinner, I'll be too stuffed to even notice his snoring. I wish I could sleep now though. I've never travelled so far. But Uncle says this is the longest trip we'll have and in the worst conditions. We're doing a mitzvah, good work, a righteous task. I've thought a lot about that since I can't sleep...not with these strangers around me. A righteous task in ominous times, he said. A mitzvah, Papa said. Before we left, when Mama looked at me and said it was a mitzvah, I knew she wasn't talking about Uncle's righteous task but my going with him, "an old man doing all that travel alone."

He would have taken a son of his own if he'd had one. He doesn't talk to Ben or Sarah that much—just me. Because I walk with him to synagogue and to study. When my father and Ben fall behind, saying hello and greeting people as soon as we come around the corner, Uncle and I just keep walking. Uncle and I walk together those extra blocks, the two of us alone. And he tells me about Auntie Tsava who died when I was four. I hardly remember her except that she always smelled like dough. I would never tell Uncle that, though. It's not a proper thing to say to someone whose wife is dead. It's something only Mama could say.

The map she gave me was folded maybe twenty times when we set off. I try to follow her folds and creases each time I put it away, but already it is crinkled and twice the size it was when she handed it to me. I have been studying it since we left, tracing the path of our journey, marked out by her in black ink. Moving away from where we live in Tykocin, a small dot on the map near Bialystok, the black ink twisting through familiar names — Suprasl, Bielsk, Krynki — and the names along our way — Augustow, Gdansk. She has circled Kutno twice, where Uncle lived with his Tsava. He says we will go there last. He says we have not a planned route so much as we are travellers going any which way we are needed and asked to come, but Mama wanted me to have the map anyways. She knew I would appreciate it. It was crisp and neat when she gave it to me, but looking at it now, wrinkled in the half-light of the winter sky, it hurts my eyes and only makes me feel more tired. I have it wedged under my dead elbow, my arm as a paperweight, and I promise myself I will not look at it again until I can do so with proper light at a proper table. I don't want to risk dropping it in the mud or losing it somewhere along the road.

———

This whole place is smaller than I expected—smaller than I'm used to. Here, the synagogue, the school, and the mikvah are all in one building. It is beautiful, though, from the outside at least. When we first saw the synagogue, I swear my jaw almost dropped. It's not like me to be so impressed, but I could see even Uncle was taking in the sight so I'm sure it was really something. He said it looks like a smaller version of the Grozdowski synagogue in Warsaw. To me it looks like a Czar's palace. Or a chapel from ancient Rome. It has four pillars in front, thick like oak trees, and a domed roof. It's made of stone, but you can tell the roof has been patched; even from the street you can see that some of its foundation is wood. Uncle says the one in Warsaw is so tall, and the dome so shiny, that you wouldn't be able to make out any of the details on the top—not unless you were high up on some other building. This shul isn't so tall. Uncle says it can't be because there is an old church near here which is so old that just like an old woman it has begun to shrink. But laws are laws and around here people pay special attention, and so our shul can be no taller than their church.

We waited on the steps for the cantor to meet us and walk us home. Uncle says I should savour every bite of food I get in the house because for the rest of our trip we'll be staying mostly in inns, and that's not the same as home cooking.

Either the cantor was late or we were early because we stood there a long time. Uncle didn't mind, but that's because he was well rested. Standing on the frozen ground seemed only to make my tired legs ache worse. He just stood there, closing his eyes, rocking back and forth, taking deep breaths, telling me to smell this new place so I could write about it later in detail in my journal. The fresh air didn't interest me, and all I could smell was cold. But then I saw Pietka. Rather, I heard him first, shouting with another boy, waving a piece of paper.

At first I thought he was young because he was the shorter of the two and quite chubby. It wasn't until the other boy walked back inside the building and Pietka kept arguing that I knew the deep voice I'd heard was his. After the other boy vanished, Pietka came and stood near us on the stairs. He was on the other side of the pillar when he lit up his cigarette. I could feel Uncle take in the smell. He opened his eyes and stared at me, as if expecting to find the source of the smell somewhere on me, smoke coming out of my ears or nose. Then he noticed Pietka and made his way around the pillar. "*Sholem-aleychem.*" Pietka took the cigarette out of his mouth and offered my uncle his hand, reciprocating his hello, "*Sholem-aleychem.*"

Pietka looked my uncle up and down. The young man from before was walking towards us. Through pressed lips, to keep the lit cigarette dangling but without dropping it from his mouth, Pietka introduced himself, "I'm Pietka and this is Tzvi." He pointed a finger at the boy, and I watched the cigarette's burning stub shake dangerously in his mouth. Tzvi stood away from us on the ground beyond the steps and smiled at my uncle. Twice Pietka's size and yet he wouldn't dare look him in the eye. His black hat and pais matched mine, the same as all the other religious boys now streaming out the doors behind him. Uncle repeated Pietka's name, its Polishness misshapen and clunky in his mouth. Finally he introduced himself and then pointed to me on the other side of the pillar. "And this is my nephew, Isaac." Pietka seemed surprised to notice me there. He shook my hand hard and smiled. "Well, we should get going. Good Shabbas to you, Isaac." And with that he and Tzvi walked away, the two of them moving quickly down the street.

Such a mismatch: tall Tzvi all in black and little Pietka in his dirty brown-cuffed trousers. Uncle didn't say anything, but I could tell he was organizing what he thought of Pietka and this place in his head. The cantor arrived and we finally headed to someplace warm. He was pointing out everything in the street and talking Uncle's ear off. I didn't listen to one word. I usually would have, but my stomach was growling and after having forgotten for a while, I remembered again how cold I was.

We finally got here only an hour ago, enough time for Uncle and the cantor to turn back around and go to the mikvah to cleanse. I was too tired to join them and said I'd rather rest. The family have left me alone in our room. I haven't been alone since we set off, and I'm enjoying every moment of it. My stomach is still growling and the smells from downstairs are making it a little hard to concentrate. But there are two soft beds here, and from the window I can see all the men returning home. Dinner should be very soon; I cannot wait.

———

Last night was the best sleep I ever had. The cantor must think I'm strange, as I barely spoke at dinner and went to bed right after. I'm sure Uncle told him I'm not shy, but that the trip must have worn me out. I got up with Uncle at sunrise this morning. I'm training myself. It helped that everyone else in the house was up, too. Because I'm a guest, the cantor's wife is letting me have some leftover karnatzel with breakfast. I think it is even better in the morning, and I dip it in my watery porridge. The cantor has four children, and they had all left for shul by the time I came downstairs. Uncle left early to meet the community council. We won't start our work until tomorrow but, as their invited guest, he will sit with the council at shul. I eat the porridge as slowly as I can to put off having to head out by myself. I'll walk with the cantor's wife, but she'll go to the women's gallery and I will have to sit by myself. It will be too crowded to find Uncle and, besides, if anyone thought I couldn't sit through services alone, I would look like a baby and it would embarrass him.

The porridge has cooled off and a pool of grotty water has settled in the crater I have shaped the slop into. I despise cold porridge, and the taste left from the karnatzel has overpowered the oats, the oil from the meat making them salty and orange. A knock on the door is a welcome distraction. The cantor's wife (she asked me to call her Luba, but it doesn't seem right) seems startled by the sound, but after a moment's hesitation answers it anyways. Pietka is there, wearing the same pants and grey wool coat as yesterday. He and the cantor's wife are the same height, they each would come up to my armpit, and while I can't see her face, I'm sure she's not smiling.

Pietka, on the other hand, is beaming. "*Shabbat shalom*. I have come to walk with Isaac to shul." Before Luba gets a chance to intervene, I grab my coat and head for the door. Anticipating our need to make a quick exit, Pietka has already stepped away from the threshold. It's not until we're a few houses down the street that we hear her close the door behind us. Pietka laughs and adjusts his cap, "I bet she was stunned when she opened the door. You knew I'd know where to find you, right? You and your uncle are big news here. Everyone would know where to find you." His bluntness unnerves me. He talks as if I were expecting him, and he is so sure sounding that I begin to wonder if maybe I had been.

I make my voice as deep as possible to try to hide my agitation, "We are going to shul, aren't we?"

Pietka laughs again; his laughter is as loud as his shouting was yesterday and comes out just as forcefully. "Of course, boy, look at me, it is Shabbat, isn't it? Where else would we be going? And with me dressed so fancy," Pietka slides open the front of his coat to reveal a lush dark brown suit jacket and vest. Unlike his pants, there isn't even the slightest hint of a wrinkle, and he runs his fingers over the delicate gold stitching, accentuated by morning light. I feel like a little kid in my plain old black suit. Apparently satisfied with my admiration, Pietka re-buttons his coat, "We'll go and then we'll leave as soon as it is over. That is unless you would rather sit at home with the cantor and his zuftig wife?" Again, Pietka seems to read my mind, adding, "Don't worry. Your uncle won't mind you're being with me. I was sure yesterday we'd hit it off."

Already we'd reached the shul, and it occurs to me that I do not know my way back to the cantor's home at all. Yesterday I had been too tired, and today too distracted, to pay any attention to the route. Though I was won over already, I readily give myself over to Pietka's logic. Seeing a cluster of men and women in raggedy clothes standing without prayer books by the door, I am convinced the shul will be too small and too crowded to find my uncle. The men and women move aside, and I squeeze into the crowded shul. In the squeeze of men, I

41

slip off my jacket and search for Pietka behind me. Out of nowhere, he appears at my side, standing only in his vest now, his heavy coat in his hands.

With the sunlight from the door, I can see yellow stains on the collar of his white shirt. Pietka tugs at his wrinkled sleeves and rolls up the frayed cuffs. His impressive jacket must be wrapped in the bundle in his arms for fear of overheating. Our shul at home has a proper second room, so the poor have somewhere inside to go, and the women's gallery is on a balcony above the men. Here we must share the same floor. There is a separate door outside the building that leads them to a section separated from us by a carved wooden wall. The wall seems thin, but you can barely hear the women at all; only the men mumble and make noise, feet shuffling on the stone floor.

Despite the crowd and my desire not to, I spot Uncle immediately. He is sitting on the bimah beside the cantor, the platform raised a child's height above the crowd. The bimah itself looks like a smaller version of the shul: a miniature miniature Grozdowski. The four pillars are made out of wood and reach up to the dome in the ceiling. From inside, you can see that the dome is lined in carved wood, which has been painted. There is a stone eagle on a pedestal above the bimah whose wings span the distance between the pillars, its pose ready to take flight. The ark behind the bimah is carved in the same style as the dome, only on it I am better able to make out the pattern: fish jumping out of a pool of water, some with the faces of other animals, like a lion painted in silver.

The bimah is raised and so while I can see him, I am certain that Uncle is not even trying to find me in this crowd of faces. He sits still beside the cantor who nods and smiles at the congregation. He sits with his eyes closed before every service as if he has already begun praying and is waiting for the rest of us to catch up. Uncle has more to say to God than the rest of us. I am sure of it.

By the time the service is over, I am glad for the cold outside. Outside it may be the dead of winter, but inside the crowded, bowing bodies and rapid moving of lips made it feel more like the worst of summer. Pietka grabs both our jackets and pulls me by the sleeve down the steps. I nearly trip I'm so happy for the fresh, cold air. He leads me quickly away from the shul and from the first trickles of the exiting crowd.

"It's as hot as the sun in there." Pietka holds the match in his cupped hand for a moment before lighting his cigarette. "We must be gluttons for punishment." He notices me staring at his cigarette, and for the first time since our meeting, his voice is flat and unfriendly, "If you tell me you don't smoke because it's *shabbas,* I'll be very disappointed. You're not as smart as I thought you were. If you tell me you don't smoke because it smells terrible and means a girl will never kiss you," Pietka pauses for

43

a quick breath of air before his laughter, "then you are far smarter." His head jerks and I watch the quivering butt cling onto the dry skin of his bottom lip. My own laughter surprises me; not as loud as Pietka's, but I see him smile again with the corner of his mouth. We slow our speed to a stroll, and I know that I never want to hear that distant tone in his voice again and am sure that the next time I do, I will have deserved it.

The rush of people on their way home has moved in around us, but in the center of the street, Pietka and I maintain our pace. The women move quickly and with purpose. They have to be home first. The men are slower, but the cold air is incentive enough to move them along. It feels powerful to take my time in the midst of this. The cold air still feels good in my lungs and the stale warmth of a home holds no allure. The walk is the thing, and I meet Pietka stride for stride.

"What were you waving at Tzvi?" Pietka adjusts his cap, pushing it down into his mess of curly hair but doesn't answer me. "Yesterday, when I saw you in the street. You were yelling at him and waving something. It seemed like a harsh way to treat your brother."

"Just because we walk home together does not make us brothers. Tzvi is not a part of my family, though he eats our food and sleeps in our beds. Never mistake him for my brother again." The sting in his tone forces blood to rush to my ears. I can feel the heat of my embarrassment and hope he doesn't turn my way. With chubby

44

hands, Pietka pats inside his winter jacket at his vest before seeming to remember that he is no longer wearing
his fancy jacket. "It was a flyer. I brought one today to
give to you. Once I knew why you and your uncle were
here, I knew you had to have one." Pietka turns to me
and smiles. My ears still red, I reach into my back pocket
and pull out the wad of paper I always keep there. It is
folded around my mother's map, which I slip into my
other hand, hoping that Pietka won't see it. "Write it?"

When Pietka sees that I keep a small pencil in my
front pocket, he laughs and asks if I haven't ever injured
myself sitting down. I laugh too and hand him the paper.
Pietka squats down and uses his thigh to write. When he
finishes scribbling, he stands up and holds the paper out
in front of me to read. Two lines, one in block-lettered
Polish and one in Hebrew: *Ein Kemach, Ein Torah.* He
folds the paper in two and wraps it around the pencil before handing it back to me and immediately picking up
his pace. Shoving my things back in my pockets, I hurry
to catch up again.

Together we walk until the streets are clear and the
afternoon sun is low enough to allow our eyes entrance
into the windows of the homes we pass. I begin to recognize buildings, storefronts, and houses. Again and
again, we turn onto streets we have walked before, this
place shrinking into familiarity. Passing street signs, I
read the names aloud until I start to anticipate the words
before the letters become clear: Mickiewicza, Skorgi,

Lubelska. Pietka tells me that Napoleon passed through here on his way to see the synagogue in Olkenik. He says that the only Jew that Napoleon even looked at was his great-great-great-grandfather, "He was the only man in the street that Napoleon could look at, eye to eye." Every time Pietka laughs, he has to readjust his cap. He, too, becomes more and more familiar: his mannerisms and the time taken between his words—his sudden spastic laughter.

It is too cold even for us now, and Pietka points me down the street and around the corner, "The cantor's house is first on that street. Hard to miss, they'll probably be looking out the window to see if you're coming."

Rounding the corner, leaving Pietka who is walking another way, moving onto Skorgi with its bread shop and tailor, I notice Pietka's jacket on a man coming towards me going the other direction. The dark chocolate colour and golden thread is unmistakable on one of the men from outside the shul. I look down at my feet and we pass in silence. I rub the curled paper in my pocket and spot the cantor's house. Pietka was right. The cantor's wife has seen me coming and opens the door before I knock. I tell her my flush is from the cold. L Clutching my cheeks in her palms, she pulls me towards the fire. "We best get you warm then."

———

"Pietka is only a nickname. You know that." Uncle wipes his reading glasses against the inside of his jacket before placing them back on his face. "Perhaps his real name is no longer good enough." I can tell he has been waiting to say something since he found out I'd spent much of yesterday with Pietka. Moving the stones has turned his black leather shoes chalky grey and sprinkled flakes of ash on his cheeks and in his hair. The old *genizah* is empty—a cupboard painted a brilliant blue, carved with fish and whales that stretches out above the ark. As we left the house this morning, Uncle told me the story of this *genizah*: in 1895, the great synagogue in Eishyshok had been burnt to the ground with the whole of the shtetl. A great many precious artefacts, all the *shemot,* papers and books sacred because the name of God is printed upon them, were lost but some survived. These were stored in a crawl space built into the foundation of a local councilman's home, entrusted to him as head of the community. While his house was destroyed with the rest of the homes, the stones surrounding the crawl space, impervious to the fire's heat, had kept the articles unharmed. The council here had taken this story as a precautionary tale and shortly after, moved all *shemot* into a *genizah* set into a stone foundation under the bimah.

It took four boys to help Uncle and me move the stones aside. Though Tzvi was not one of them, I saw him standing by the doors when we came in. He waved at me, but I looked away. Uncle saw and made a special point to go over and shake his hand. After the others left, he asked why I behaved so poorly. I told him I couldn't explain why; I just don't like Tzvi. That was when Uncle shook his head and began talking about Pietka.

"Tzvi was sent here to study and has been living with Pietka's family. According to our host, Pietka has been giving him a hard time since he arrived." I only shrug, but he doesn't stop. "You don't know him. Not well enough. And I'm afraid you are maybe too young to understand his way of thinking. He has dangerous politics. Dangerous ideas make for dangerous men."

It is the first time Uncle has ever treated me like a child... ever. If I am too young, why am I here—not some silly child following him around. "I know why we're here, Uncle." My own voice, sudden and sure, startles us both. Uncle stretches up to his full height. A shower of dust falls from his trousers. Leaning on one of the wooden pillars of the bimah, he crosses his arms and bows his head to look into my face. I realize my hands are twisted into fists by the feel of my nails scratching my palms. "I know why you were asked to come here. Mama told me about that night, about politics. I know what danger is, dangerous ideas and dangerous men. Pietka is not one of them." I shake the fingers loose from my own grip, aware and unable to stop every muscle under my skin from gently quivering.

Uncle reaches his hand out and places it on my arm, "I know you do." With the weight of his thick hand on my sleeve, we crouch together into the mess of papers at our feet. His touch is my relief. I pull a book from the stone cove, dust the cover with my sleeve and hold it towards him. Uncle's hand slips from my arm to take the book and place it on the pile with the rest. "When we have removed enough, I'll have to go through everything, and I'll need your help to prepare what's needed for burial." I nod, relieved. The air between us having calmed, my ease returns. I pass over to him a collection of papers loosely bound by a leather spine. Flipping it open and sliding his thumb down the blotched ink on the first page, Uncle sighs, "*Genizot* are not only for the storing of *shemot*. The book of Proverbs was once placed in a *genizah* as a work of heresy. The purpose, you see, is to preserve the good things from harm and the bad things from harming."

———

It seems like Pietka has been avoiding me since we first walked together. I tell myself it is because he knows I got into trouble for being with him. I keep his note—the flyer he wrote for me in the street—in my pocket all the time in case. My pockets bulge with the map, my own pencil and notes, and Pietka's message. My journal I keep tucked into my vest. I would leave these things in our room but for my fear that one of the cantor's young children will discover the papers and wreck them, or worse, present them to their father.

49

A few times, I have read some of my notes to my uncle, including thoughts or things I have learned and observations about this place. The map and the note, however, are private. It feels like Mama's map or Pietka's words would dry up on the page if anyone else saw them and become nothing more than loose powder that used to mean something. I will worry less when we move on; in two days we leave this shtetl for our next destination. Uncle and I will be staying at an inn. There, my things can be kept safe behind a locked door, being items of no consequence or interest to strangers. There, Pietka's words won't mean so much; here they feel like stones in my pocket. The paper I have read over many times. The Polish letters I can only recognize and sound out a little, but the Hebrew is simple. That is, the words are simple, but I can tell from their weight on me that their meaning is not.

After three days of helping Uncle sort books and papers, watching him read and grapple with his chore, I have an afternoon to myself. Uncle knows I will seek out Pietka, but he didn't say or do anything to try to stop me. Pietka's house is not hard to find; yesterday I followed Tzvi home from the shul. I followed him around the corner and saw him enter a small wooden home on the street right behind the shul. Unlike the cantor's home which is brick and dark, Pietka's house is one floor and painted bright yellow. The whole thing is made of wood which can be seen beneath the strips of peeling paint.

Every house on the street has a number painted on the door; Pietka lives at number thirty-six. "*Chai,*" I think as I knock on the door. "Life." I hear someone coming and catch his name in my throat; I must remember to ask for Chaim here. The woman who answers must be Pietka's mother, and she tells me that he is at work and sends me to the tailor whose sign I had walked by and read so many times the other day.

The tailor is too busy to fuss with me; at the mention of Pietka's name, he waves me out through his shop, out the back, and into the dirt alley behind where I find Pietka unloading a horse. I can barely recognize him at first; his muffler is pulled up to cover his face and he has another one wrapped over his head to cover his ears. He doesn't hear me call his name, so I wait for him to notice me rather than be startled by a tap on the shoulder. I am dressed for the windy winter weather, hoping that Pietka and I could take one of our walks.

"Hello again." Even with his face covered I can tell he is smiling.

"I want you to tell me what it means." I had planned to start with a friendly hello but inside there is an urgency I had not expected. We will have all afternoon to walk and talk, but I don't feel like I can without knowing first. *No flour, no Torah.* Pietka's riddle for me. I am pulled under by the feeling that he has left me alone to have time to tease out its meaning and I have failed. "I have been so busy helping my uncle in the synagogue, but I have the paper on me in case I would see you and you could explain it to me. Since, that is, you made it sound like there was something to explain."

"Her name is Mara," he says petting the mare's ear. "The tailor calls her 'donkey.' But Mara is what I named her so that's what she's called. Mara and I go to the farms around here to collect and drop off work for the tailor." Pietka gently tugs the reins. Mara sweeps her head in broad strokes side to side in response. "Let's get her out of the cold." Together we begin to walk to a large stable that houses the livestock of the local merchants: heavyset horses, squat mules, work animals. Pietka rubs Mara under her leather straps. "We'll put you to sleep with the other workers." He then he looks at me. "Will you be here for the holidays?"

"No, we leave in two days. Our work here is pretty much done. We bury tomorrow."

"And everything else?" I look at Pietka, startled. "Things that are buried can be dug up."

Surprised, I tell him, "We burn tomorrow night."

Chuckling, Pietka pats Mara heavily on the shoulder, "Small town. Don't be so surprised I knew what you were doing."

"Tzvi tells the cantor you've been giving him a hard time."

"Tzvi tells the cantor, and then the cantor tells your uncle, who tells you. Such gossip." Pietka pulls the muffler down under his chin and rubs his hand between the wool and his neck. "I have five sisters, Isaac, did you know that?"

"No. I only have one."

"Five unmarried sisters, one mother, one father, myself, and one Tzvi. Eight people in one home. And not just when Tzvi showed up, there has always been a Tzvi, a religious boy that needed someone else's bed to sleep in, and someone else's food to eat. Since I was little, my father has done the right thing and invited these boys the council sends over into his home." The stable doors are thick wood with hanging iron chains that scrape the ground as we push them open. In her stall, Mara presses her forehead against Pietka's shoulder as he begins to unhook and pull off her straps. She has to lean so far down that it looks as if all of her weight is resting on him. "Soon there will only be seven. My oldest sister is leaving to live with my aunt and her husband. She's going there to help take care of his elderly parents." Stroking her skin, Pietka eases the yoke from off Mara's neck.

I don't move, not wanting him to stop talking. Pietka leans against the stall door. "My father works all day, out in the cold, stopping only for lunch and prayer. He comes home, hands bleeding and rough from the wind, and Tzvi, who has never carried a load heavier than one or two books, eats his food. My sisters have no dowry, and Tzvi has them ironing his shirts." *Ein Kemach, Ein Torah.* Pietka's father works so that Tzvi can eat; Pietka's father feeds him so that Tzvi can learn. "Ein Kemach, ein Torah.

No bread, no Torah." Pietka's voice echoes my thoughts, but the words are moved by anger, "Studying holy books is no longer enough."

I turn what he has said over and over in my brain, the words being ones I have traced under my fingers for days. My own place, my own hands, never sore, never bleeding. We leave the stable in silence. Each shuffling in our own thoughts, Pietka moves ahead of me.

Even though I am at least six inches taller and with longer legs, I fall behind him, happy not to have him, for the moment, see my face. It is the way it has always been; it is no longer enough. Again, my own frustration forces me to keep talking, "He said you had dangerous politics. That those words were political."

Pietka stops walking and allows for me to catch up. He doesn't look at me, or I at him, but we start off again, this time at equal speed. "Everyone here knows my politics, Isaac." His voice is quieter than it has ever been. Still, I don't dare turn my head. "Next year in Palestine, next year in Palestine. But where in the holy books, with all their rabbinical ramblings, does it say how to plant farmland? Or build homes? Those are not the men to settle a country. A homeland. It will be the labourers, the horses and the donkeys of the old country that will break land in the new. And what of politics? What are politics when you refuse to speak any language other than your own? How influential can you be then?" For a few minutes, we are just to men pacing the streets, and I nod my head as I repeat his words, "Next year in Palestine indeed."

―――

Plum woolen blankets have been thrown over the hard wood seats of the open carriage. At first it looked as if Uncle would be rocked to sleep again, his eyes closed and his shoulder slumped over the side of the wagon. But the wheels caught on a branch, and he was jarred by the strong jerk of gravity trying to snag his body out of the wagon. Now he is fully awake and watching me. This new distance between Uncle and I can be measured in the length of Pietka's words tucked into the bottom of my satchel; his words sitting buried under socks and pants. "Perhaps I was too quick to judge your friend, to place him in the company of dangerous men." My toes curl inside my boot, stubs of flesh and bone tensing and releasing, begging him to stop. "He's a thinker, at least. It is the ones that don't think you have to be wary of. The ones too crude to bother." The wagon moves smoothly down the road but my stomach lurches, twisting and hot. Pietka's words, my hearing them, a betrayal of him — my uncle — now sitting so close and watching so carefully. "I'm glad we left today." I turn my head and will my eyes to plead with him for silence, "I was ready to go." He scoops the edge of the wool blanket off the empty seat beside him and drapes it across our knees.

"It's a short trip. You'll have just begun to feel as if you've left when you'll realize you have actually just arrived."

§

Jake unwrapped the scarf from his neck and wondered again if he had made a mistake, gone about this whole thing the wrong way. He had hesitated on the phone, not sure what he would tell the old man if he asked why he was calling. Jake had spoken his name and then that of his father into the receiver and heard nothing, no hints of recognition from the other end of the line. "Ike, Isaac Langley." Still nothing. "I think you two knew each other from Poland."

Chaim coughed loudly into the phone and cleared his throat. "Langley isn't a Jewish name." The words were an accusation.

"He changed it," Jake answered and gave him the last name as it had been, as it had been before. He had begun again to search for the words to explain, in brief, why he had called but the old man interrupted, "You can come see me. I'll give you my address." He lived in a duplex off Fleet Street, in Ike's own neighbourhood.

Now, standing in the cold, sweating under his winter coat, Jake wondered if he should be doing this at all: bothering a stranger and for what he wasn't sure. He had considered bringing the folder, all of it, with him but it felt wrong. Like a violation of his father's privacy though he couldn't quite decipher how or why it felt that way. Instead, he brought the single artefact in the folder which bore the strange man's name: a scrap of newspaper, a letter addressed "Dear Editor" and signed "C.P. Yanofsky, Canadian." Jake felt for the scrap in his pocket.

The sound of several locks being opened, one by one, came to him from the other side of the door. He could hear the sound of old fingers fumbling with a chain and then the pop of the seal of the door being broken. Chaim was covering his mouth with a white handkerchief. It hung like a cotton pyramid down from two fingers on his left hand which held it pressed over his top lip. "Come in." The cotton billowed out with his voice, its ironed-in creases still stiff. "I caught a flu this winter." Jake stepped into the house and Chaim closed the door behind him, "This winter. Every winter." With his right hand, Chaim slipped the chain back into its slot on the door frame and turned the lock. The door was also fitted with a fat dead bolt, plated in gold. Jake nodded and slipped off his shoes. "Bad lungs," said Chaim as he held out his right hand towards Jake, who shook it and smiled.

"Mr. Yanofsky, it's very nice to meet you."
Chaim let his left hand and his handkerchief drop to his side. "You too, Jacob. Son of Isaac." He looked Jake up and down then gestured with his hand again, "Come in." Jake followed him into the formal living room, "Thank you for meeting me." The man waved his hand over his shoulder without turning around. "Have a seat. I made tea."

Chaim went through a narrow doorway into the kitchen while Jake surveyed his options for seating. The room was well furnished. The long couch which sat against the wall had a high back and arched arms. The shape and fabric matched two oversized chairs which sat across the room on either side of the fireplace. The coffee table in front of the couch was heavy dark wood, and had on it two mugs resting on silver coasters. Jake sat down in front of one of the mugs. The bottom cushion of the couch had a plastic cover on it which crackled when he sat down. Jake raised himself slightly with his hands and pushed back further on the couch, pressing on the plastic and causing an encore of the uncomfortable sound.

Chaim returned, carrying a large tea pot hidden under a cow-shaped potholder. "Mmm," he said and nodded towards the couch. He poured tea into each mug, right up to the brim, and then set the pot down in the middle of the table, on top of the bovine. "It was the style once. My daughters insist I take them off, but the zipper won't go anymore." He lifted his mug and coaster. Jake leaned forward, sure that the tea would spill and burn Chaim's fingers. But the old man's hands were perfectly steady, and he set his load down again on the corner of the coffee table without spilling a drop and sat in one of the high-backed chairs.

"When I called your sister by accident, I was sure I had called the wrong number."

"She told me. But she recognized it. You trying to use an old nickname. My middle name is Pinchas, and when I met your father, I went by Pietka."

Chaim was short, even by Eastern European Jewish standards. The top of his head was bald, but a laurel of dark grey hair crowned him at the temples. His ears were large and the skin off his lobes hung down like tear drops. He had thick eyebrows, the hairs of which were long and curled, which squatted low over his eyelids. In his late eighties, Chaim held his broad shoulders straight and firm across his back, only slouching slightly when he bent to take hold of his tea, which he drank while steam still rose off the cup. Jake, on the other hand, waited for the dark liquid to cool, taking the time to tell Chaim about his father's death and the basement and what he had found there. The old man listened closely, emptying his mug all the while, in what seemed like one long, never ending sip. He then put it back on its coaster and crossed his arms over his stomach, before asking, "How did he go?"

"Oh," Jake fondled his mug on its coaster, "congestive heart failure. He was fine for a long time. "

"And for how long not fine?"

"Umm, four months. Five maybe. But a lot of it, like painwise, was controllable so..." Jake let the tip of his thumb dip into the amber tea which was still warm. He blotted his thumb dry against his lips.

"Of all the ways to go," Chaim waved a lined fingertip at Jake, "there are more than you should think, so I suppose that isn't too bad. Better for the family. You, your mother, brothers, sisters."

"My mother passed away a long time ago."

Chaim pressed a finger into his chest, "My Ruth, too."

"It's just me, actually."

"Just you? Just one?" The rise in his voice was met with

an outbreak of coughing, the white handkerchief instantly re-
appearing from somewhere up his sleeve. When it was over,
Chaim pushed the cotton back into his sweater. "I was one of
so many, I never got to say, 'just me.' I don't like the sound of
it."

Jake smiled despite himself, "You get used to it."

"I bet you do." A painful chuckle and another cleared
throat, "Your mother. I never met her." Chaim chewed on his
flat bottom lip. "To tell you all of it, I only saw your father once
here. We talked on the phone a little, over the years here and
there, around the holidays. But we saw each other only once,
later. We lived in the same city but..." He rolled his hands in
the air in front of him, the palms of his hands looking soft
and worn. "With us," he gestured to the room around them,
"we came to one new country, came out of it but maybe on
two sides of a world."

Jake reached into his pocket and took out the newspaper
clipping. He unfolded it and leaned over, offering it to Chaim.
"I found this in his folder. I'm not sure where or when it's
from."

Chaim took the paper from him and held it up close in
front of his eyes, aged newsprint dangling, again, from two
fingers. "Do you know your history?" Jake hadn't time to answer before the old man set the clipping down in his lap.
"'None is too many.' I wrote this to the editor sometime in,"
he squinted, the lines around his eyes twitching with the effort, "1967." Chaim opened his eyes and folded the clipping,
"Some idiot complaining about immigration laws, change.

Said there were too many cracks in the system already." He chewed his lip and tucked the clipping under his coaster, "Leaks, he meant. For people like us to get through." Leaning back into his chair, Chaim pointed at the folded newsprint, "Did you want that back?"

Jake shook his head no, "Means more to you than it does to me."

"Makes sense your father would keep it."

"It does?"

"I flatter myself. That," he pointed again, "is how your father found me." Chaim looked into Jake's still-full mug. "Milk?"

"No thanks, it's fine. I just like to let it cool off." Jake picked up the lukewarm tea, pausing with the cup in front of his mouth. "You said two sides of the world." He took a sip.

And so Chaim explained, his speech punctuated here and there by a dry rumble like gravel caught in his throat. "After," he waved his hand in the air, signalling a time and event no single word could every truly stand for, "I went to Palestine. I wanted to be a settler. I had always wanted to, but then it was a time when I did not feel like I maybe had a choice. It was the one place in the world. And right away, I met my wife and had three kids and did all of that. My sisters had come here instead. I had two who survived, and Ruth and I with our kids came to see them. Ruth was like you now, just one. So she asked if we couldn't stay here, and then she could have sisters too. I didn't want to leave Israel yet, but she asked me and so what could I do? We came here. Became Canadian and Israeli.

My children, boy and the both girls, all went back for the army. You don't fight for a home and someone else will."

Jake nodded, "That's good to remember."

"Always. But then that is my side of the world."

———————

It was because he'd never been there before that he was late. He'd seen it from the road of course, the oversized red pagoda beams curled skyward over the paved parking lot. Such flourish for such a dump and the only direction his old friend had given: "the Ruby Foo's Diner, inside the hotel. It is hard to miss." So he explained that he was late because he had gotten lost, all those one ways, back streets, and one tiny parking lot entrance. That and the driving; he never got used to driving on the wide interweaving roads, the dips and rises on and off the expressway. On Décarie, other cars could honk all they wanted, and he would just wave them around, smiling and swearing under his breath; "*Tuches arine,* that's right. Maniacs." But he was happy to come, more than happy to come. Though it was true, he hadn't recognized Ike at first.

"Should I have? You look so different."

"I know better than to take that as a compliment."

Chaim laughed and undid the cuffs on his shirt sleeves, "You have striking cheek bones, Yitzhak. I never had the chance to notice before what with the *pais*." He took a moment to reconcile this dapper man—a few years younger than he was—with the boy he remembered.

"Well, you sound the same and look like Pietka. Just older."

"Much older." Chaim laughed again, generously like he always had, so unlike Ike whose even softest chuckle sounded caught in his throat. "And no silly names, please, even if for old times' sake." A squat waitress, her full hips almost the width of the table, saddled up to the old friends and put down two cups of coffee. Chaim ordered a matzo ball soup, which she scribbled on her notepad before turning to Ike who shook his head to indicate he would have nothing.

"Not hungry? Or should I not trust the food?"

Chaim looked around the room: mainly empty booths, a smattering of men in suits and hats eating alone. The diner was almost brand new, yet it already wore a dingy air as though a place meant for men and women speaking in hushed tones. "I don't spend much time in this neighbourhood. Though my Ruth wants to move; St. Laurent is too far out for her taste."

"Not familiar with this area? You don't visit the cemetery enough."

Chaim sipped his coffee and shrugged. "Eventually I'll get to visit forever."

The waitress returned and set the bowl of soup on the table. Broth sloshed over the rim, creating a deep yellow moat on the saucer. She turned and left without asking if there was anything else they needed, like a soup spoon. Chaim wiped his teaspoon, once dipped in coffee, on the thin napkin and slid it into the bowl.

He ate while they caught up. Chaim talked about the move from Israel, his children, "Asher, Danika and Talia, all smart and all lazy." Ike, in turn, described his pregnant wife, their first, and how nervous she got "every time there is a move or a push. She counts moments in time between each kick, anxious until it moves again. I tell her over and over that the baby is just asleep." He didn't mention, didn't say why he too held his breath until the baby moved again. And then there were those other details, the formalities of old friends meeting so far away from where they came. Questions answered without asking, well-worn answers given in a word or two.

Ike watched Chaim eat, impressed with himself that he could see and recognize, even after all that time, the way his old friend carefully chose his words. Each sentence Chaim uttered, no matter the topic, was full of words specifically chosen for some real purpose. Chaim remembered and recognized too; Ike was thinking, trying to read his face when he should have just been listening to what he said. There is comfort in finding out that some things never changed.

Halfway through his soup, Chaim, sweating in the sticky summer heat, rolled the the cuffs of his sleeves. Built like a pit bull, his wrists — thick and as wide as his forearms — were now exposed to the gently air-conditioned room. The single rotating fan that sat on the windowsill cooled the beads of sweat that had all the while been running down his neck. He let his arms rest, palm down, on the chill lino tabletop.

"I swear it's hotter here than in the desert."

"I wouldn't know but I would doubt it."

"It is because the heat here, trapped between all the brick buildings, is out of place. The city does not know how to let itself breathe." He signalled to the waitress for some water. "Summer is the only time of year my kids stop to complaining about the move. They love it and I spend three months sweating. Ruth has time to do nothing. She spends three months washing and starching my shirts."

"Well, you dress too formal maybe," said Ike, eyeing his friend's thick woven cotton. "A dress shirt on a day like today." Ike sat almost smug in his light summer shirt, long sleeved but thin enough to make out the lines of the undershirt worn underneath. Rose had bought it for him, picked it out especially to show off his tan. That summer, like every summer, the two of them were spending their weekends in the backyard. Usually, Ike sat in the shade reading, and Rose let her body bake in the sun. But that year was different. Ike spent his days under his wife's watchful eye, baby-proofing the yard while, pregnant, she sat hiding from even the slightest vestige of heat. The house gave great shade while it loomed like a brick-laid oven behind them.

Chaim flipped his arms over, his knuckles now resting on the cool hard surface before using his right hand to tug at the fabric in the armpit of his shirt and run his finger around the collar. "I know, summer is unbearable in these," he said, straightening his right elbow and raising his forearm, "but they are the only shirts that cannot see through."

The numbers were blurred at the edges as if the ink was trying to escape, seep further into the skin, spread out and mark the whole body...the whole man. A sorrow born somewhere beyond the depth of his own thinking pulled at the skin on Ike's face. His arms, both of them, sat naked in his airy sleeves. "I could see why you'd want to hide it."

Chaim pulled his arms in, close to his chest. "Hide it, no." He shook his head and rubbed the stubble that speckled his wide chin. "Cover it so people do not stare so much maybe. Keep it to myself."

"Still, it can't be comfortable."

"Would I *schvitz* like a *hazer* if it were?" But that wasn't what Ike had meant and they both knew it. Chaim shrugged, "More discomfort for strangers than for me. I've had time to get used to it there. Before I would be able to close my eyes and read the number off the inside of my eyelids. Like a sunspot, something burned in, but now..." He shrugged again. "Listen, my eldest Danika says that when she gets married, she wants to do it outside on a beach in Tel Aviv, and I have to be there in short sleeves. She is not happy at the idea of me sweating in the pictures."

Ike tipped his coffee cup, closed one eye, and looked into the stained porcelain. With a clink he returned it to its saucer and pushed the pair to the edge of the table to signal for a refill. Chaim waited for his friend to speak but was rewarded with nothing. "Isaac, you are right. Sometimes I lie a little to myself. But some of us lie a lot. Maybe it's not something to hide but not something I want to show off either." The peach apron was making its way towards their booth. Cups were filled with hot coffee from a fresh pot and the soup bowl was cleared.

"Better safe. Better safe than sorry." The words were a mantra Ike spoke as he stirred sugar into his cup. "Better than to be foolish. Better that than tempt the beast." The spoon rocked back and forth as it rested against the saucer, "Better sweaty than stared at."

Each man took a hold of his drink, Ike sipping with caution, so as not to burn his tongue, and Chaim pouring the steamy brew easily over his lips.

"We sat together, same table, same room. But not in the same place." Chaim pressed his hands into a tepee in his lap. "My side of the world and his. Me," the old man pointed with outstretched fingers to his own chest, "still a Zionist. Him, Ike Something-or-other."

The afternoon had begun to wear on, and Jake sat listless on the couch. All the nervous tension that had wound itself tightly inside him since finding Chaim a few days earlier had been snipped free at the first mention by the other man of his father's name. It sat loose, uncoiled inside his skin. Jake had done his best to follow while Chaim spoke, drifting from one story to another: something about a diner and his father, summer's heat, and his own life as it had panned out after 1938 when Ike and Chaim had met. He had done his best to listen, but the old man's words were heavy, and they sat inside of him now like a pile of stones on top of what he already knew.

The way his father lived, the way he had acted with his mother's friends. The house in such a Jewish neighbourhood and Jake's small bar mitzvah, both concessions to Rose even though the latter took place after she had died.

"My kids, now, none of them live here. I moved to Montreal so they could be near family and when they got older, they all left and stayed away." Chaim was no more a believer in conversational transitions than in uncomfortable silences. "My sister stays in a nursing home near here. So convenient for them when they visit. In and out, they come and go." Shifting his weight and lowering his head, so that his flat feet rocked forward on the carpet, Chaim rose in one easy movement. Leaving the cups behind, he picked up the newspaper clipping and gestured for Jake to follow as he headed back into the kitchen.

"I had five sisters once, and then two. Now one." The kitchen was bright, a large window almost the height of the room let in light from the rectangular yard. Jake looked out; the snow was flat and clean; only a short path of footsteps along the side of the house had disturbed it. The track led to a small pool of yellow grass where the mouth of a tin gutter had melted the snow. "That is not what is supposed to happen. I went from one of the oldest to the very youngest in just sixty years." Chaim picked a plum out of the fruit bowl which sat on the wooden island and fished his hand in a cutlery drawer. Pulling out a short knife, he sliced into the unripened fruit, twisting the two halves around the pit with sticky fingers. "It is not how time works that it should go backwards." The plum gave way and Chaim bit the smaller half, without the pit, in two. Jake stood across from him. "Danika and Talia were two of my sisters' names. We would have used more but we had a boy."

"I'm named after a great uncle."

"I know." Chaim ate another purple piece, sucking the juice off of his bottom lip. When he chewed, all the skin on his face moved up and down so that Jake could both watch and hear the effort. "And your aunts and uncles? Your father had at least one brother I remember."

"A brother and a sister."

"What happened to them?"

"Died, then, but I think that's about all he knew. My mother heard once that his sister was near Warsaw for a while. I'm not sure. It wasn't his favourite topic."

Unlike her husband, Rose had always liked talking about the dead. They had become, in her teenage years, familiar company. She said she preferred to think of the absent dead than have to remember the living dead: the strangers' faces she could still recall, slack bodies moving around her, sleeping near her, blank faces. She could not speak of that but told Jake she was lucky, being separated from her family so early on. Her memories of them were not touched by anything else - not touched by what happened next.

Jake was always an eager audience. He pictured all the women in her stories with his mother's face: a grandmother who never went out for the evening without wearing a beautiful red hat pinned with a soft plume of red feather, who travelled Europe with her two daughters, each one with her own full set of matching luggage. A great grandfather who pulled a friend, an old man he knew, off a cargo train while a soldier was not looking. Rose's stories were set in a Europe he could picture that looked and sounded like downtown Montreal. "Hungary," Rose would say, "was different then. Like Paris now." Her family were Jews who looked and acted like him; not strange like his father's family who would have worn *tzitzit* and beards.

The young Jake couldn't picture the country his father came from. When he tried, it was always miserable and rainy, uneven dirt roads, dirt rags for clothing, the blood pink borscht his mother sometimes made. All details gleaned from an overactive imagination. Ike wouldn't talk about it. Whenever his son asked about Poland, he was given the same reply: "Why do you want to know about that place? It does not belong to you. You are no more Polish now than I ever was." Then Ike would sulk, push the boy at his mother and disappear again. Only she could calm Ike when he got that way, holding his hand to her cheek, his cheek to her hand. She would speak to him softly in Yiddish, letting her knuckles massage the meat of his face.

It had been Rose who told Jake that he had had an aunt and uncle: his father's sister Sarah and brother Benjamin. Rose told Jake that he was named after a great uncle, his father's favourite. "And your *tate* was his favourite too, of all the whole family." As a Jewish child, you are not so much given a name as you are invited to share it. Jake wanted to know what happened to his father's family; after all, he was connected to them in name, both first and last. And Jake had asked, more than once. He couldn't help it. When he asked, his father's face would flush at the temples. He would press his tightened fists on the table, flexing them again and again. The words would be placed into the empty air in front of him and not right at Jake. Ike wouldn't look at Jake. *I don't know,* he would say, *I wasn't there.* Never more than that. No matter how he asked, how badly he wanted to know, Ike wouldn't talk about it, wouldn't bleed on his son.

"My mother told me to stop asking him. She said it hurt him, even made him cry, but I never saw that."

"Just like Isaac," Chaim chewed the last bits of fruit flesh from the plum's bumpy core and then threw the naked pit into the garbage. He cleared his throat. "So controlled. Even in anger."

"I think I wanted him to be happy that I wanted to know." Absentmindedly, Jake flattened the hair at the nape of his neck with the pads of his fingers. He let his hand rest there, cupping the crook between his shoulder and his neck. "I never really got it. He didn't even like being around when my mom talked about her family and what she went through. He just didn't want to hear it."

"Listen Jacob, they are the ones who did everything. But it's us — those of us who managed to survive were the ones who came out with all the guilt."

A cloud moved in the sky and the kitchen was, for a moment, cast grey in its shadow. Chaim looked at the young man,

71

let his eyes rest on the thirty-six-year-old's face — a son, someone else's son, not yet even his own boy's age. Then, the light returned. The boy looked up and the man looked away.

There was time for another cup of coffee but then both men would have to go. Each was expected elsewhere: Ike back at the store and Chaim at a music recital. Three cups and the reunion would be done. He had been happy to see Chaim, a remnant from another life, but was growing anxious to leave. Chaim didn't seem to notice.

"It's nice to see a familiar face here. That's not something we," Chaim tapped a plastic button on his shirt and then pointed across the table, "get to do very often. Reminisce."

Ike shrugged, "We've all been places we don't want to remember."

Leaning over the surface of the table, resting on his elbows, Chaim gripped a meaty fist around the forearm of his sleeve. "And you?"

"Too many places to remember. But none of them with a guard at a gate."

"Who ever said it took a guard to make a prison?"

Ike's face twitched in embarrassment. His was the shame of being found out mixed with a kind of jealousy too awful to speak out loud, even to himself. "You know," he said, playing with the handle on his cup, "As soon as I read that letter and saw your name, I was sure even without thinking that it had to be you. What are the odds, but I could just tell."

"Really? Well." Chaim chuckled but Ike couldn't bring himself to smile. "And how was that?"

Ike rubbed the underside of the table with his hands and nodded slowly. His voice low, he looked at his old friend. "You were always so loud it scared me."

———

Chaim chewed the last of his plum before speaking. "Some people find it easier when you let them forget who you are, why you might be different." Chaim shrugged and looked at the newspaper clipping. "Some people prefer to let them forget." He handed the creased newsprint to Jake. "On second thought, you keep it."

———

The winter air, a sky gone dark for at least an hour, sharpened the shapes and colours Jake passed as he drove down the street. It would be a miserable night to find a spot along Rue Guy, which would already be heavily lined with cars doing their best not to slide down the icy street. Jake knew Seda was waiting for him in the restaurant, her favourite. The novelty of breakfast food — omelettes, waffles, crepes — for a grown-up meal like dinner was a ritual which never ceased to please her. Jake knew she would wait patiently until they had both ordered and drinks arrived at the table before asking him how it went. He knew she wouldn't press him for details, waiting instead for what he wanted to share to trickle out of him, over hours and days, as it always did. Seda's excitement for his meeting Chaim had balanced Jake's apprehension. But unlike him, she was still waiting.

Jake could tell her what he learned about his father's trip in '38, when Ike had been only fifteen. He could tell her about Chaim and what he was like and what he told Jake about meeting his father. When Jake was at the doorway, preparing to leave, Chaim had asked him if he had gotten everything he needed. "Was there anything else?"

Jake's face grew warm, he was silly for not having thought more about it beforehand — for not coming in with a better idea of what he wanted to hear. He slipped his arms into the lined sleeves of his coat and buttoned it all the way to the throat.

Chaim stood across from him in the vestibule, holding Jake's scarf. "We could have talked more about then, when your father was a teenager. You could come again."

"Thanks," Jake took the cotton scarf out of the old man's hands and slipped it over his head, "I might take you up on that. Though, I think I'm good. I mean, it's enough."

Chaim clapped his hands together, rubbing the rough skin of his palms against each other, "Well, okay then."

"I guess..." Jake hesitated. The wondering behind the question had hit his lips before the exact words to express it. "The papers. What do you think they did with the papers?"

"Oh." The white handkerchief, draped over a stubby finger, rubbed back and forth against his nose, "Some buried but mostly burned." Chaim sniffled and sighed. "Better your great-uncle's fire than theirs..."

––––––––––

The restaurant was warm and cozy which was why Seda loved eating there. Bright country-kitchen style lighting hung low over the tables and bounced off the shiny painted decorations on the yellow walls: a bouquet of raspberries, a happy jug of blended fruit cocktail. It was usually busy, though at dinner it was less so. During the day, the low dividing walls between booths and tables only added to the packed-in feeling; at night, however, it possessed nothing of the bustle that animated most downtown restaurants. All the good eating spots in Montreal were perpetually congested. That's how you knew where you were, what city you were in: boisterous crowds talking over each other, no such thing as inside voices or waiting your turn.

That night, though, Jake wasn't much in the mood for crowds. He couldn't bear the thought of sitting in an over-stuffed dining room, way too close to the heads of the couple at the next table who could look over and loudly comment whenever they felt his table's food was arriving faster than theirs.

Jake hadn't expected how good it would feel to see Seda sitting there waiting for him, patient and relaxed, reading the history of the restaurant off the printed paper placemat. He couldn't help but smile.

Seda watched Jake dip another strawberry into the boat of double cream. She had been quiet the whole time while he talked about his day, nodding thoughtfully between bites of food. Jake for the most part had played with his food, moving fruit around the plate with his fork and pre-cutting each individual bite of his waffles. When he was done, he fell silent and after a moment or two began devouring his meal, as if having emptied himself of so many words, he had to fill the blank space up as quickly as possible.

"He sounds nice. Kinda how I pictured him."

"How'd you do that?"

Seda raised her shoulders and held them there, dropping her head to one side, "I dunno. Like your dad." She began plucking the crust off of her toast. "So what else did he tell you? What happened to him? You didn't say." Sweeping with her fingertips, she brushed the crumbs off the table into a cupped hand. "During the war."

Jake looked at her, stuck somewhere between confusion and surprise. "The Holocaust? He was in a concentration camp." He said it bluntly, like the answer was obvious and the question obtuse.

"Thank you, I know that." Hers was a tone that confirmed she had heard his. "Besides, you alluded to it. I just meant..."

"Specifically?" He raised his eyebrows.

Seda adjusted her expression to mimic his. "Yes, *specifically* what happened. You didn't ask?"

Jake felt something like guilt begin to pool around his feet, rising up his body. It was hot and familiar. He felt it flood his cheeks as he searched for an answer. He felt embarrassed, sorry. "I don't know."

"Oh." The word came out extra short.

"Well," he said, shoving another forkful of waffle into his face, "you don't just come out and ask that. Like, in casual conversation. 'Hey, would you mind being more specific about the painful details of your past?'" This guilt was not his.

"I don't think it's that bad a question. And I don't think he sounds like the type of person who would have minded."

"It's just not..." Jake adjusted the angle of his placemat and napkin while searching for exactly what he wanted to say. "I just didn't."

"But how could you not? Given what you were talking about? I bet your father asked when they met up." She sopped her crustless toast in a pool of hazelnut syrup.

The muscles along his jaw clenched, "He would have had the right to ask."

"The right? Like it's a secret."

"It's different." He began to feel the cream and fruit mixing in his belly. Jake dropped his head and massaged his forehead with his fingertips, pinching the skin into peaks between his eyes.

When they were first dating, Seda told Jake that one of the things she liked most about him were his hands. Yes, they were broad and masculine, he knew that, had heard it before. But she explained it was the way he used them. Despite their size, it was his fingertips he used more than anything else. Everything in his world, including himself, including her, was held like it was fragile, like thin paper that could disintegrate just from his touch. Ever since, he would catch her watching his hands. He could feel her watching them in this moment too.

"You're not getting it," he added. "Just drop it."

Rather than see, he heard her lean back and fold her arms over her chest. Felt her take a deep, steadying breath.

"I'm not getting what exactly?"

"The whole thing. What it's like. For him." Each word lay between them like a brick, the making of a wall. "Losing everything, your family, your home. A past." It was easy, this masonry, came naturally; it was in his nature. He had learned it well and had done it before. "A country."

"Please." Seda hunched low over her plate, leaning, with her head, across their dinner. She held herself in front of him, "I get it better than you ever did until apparently today." Her breath was hot and syrup sweet. Jake looked up, "Despite everything else, that was something your dad and I always had in common. And he may have hated me, but he wouldn't have forgotten that."

"He didn't hate you." Jake reached for her hand under the table, "You scared him."

———

Arriving home, he watched her disappear, frustrated, down the hallway to the bedroom. She left the door open so he could follow. Or not. Her coat dropped along the way: gloves, a scarf, a path of wool and cotton. Instead, Jake shoved his fists into his pockets and turned towards the kitchen, alone.

Hours later, into the night, he knew that if he moved softly under the sheets, he could reach her, lie with her next to him. No matter how angry, her sleepy body would forget to pull away from his touch. With warm hands firm on her hips, he whispered into her hair: "I'm sorry."

Bending her elbow, smooth forearm grazing the knuckles of his hand, she reached behind her own head to touch his cheek. "Who's next?" Pitch black, he could only feel her foot move beneath the covers to find him. Arching, she held his foot cupped in hers.

Rather than answer, Jake pressed his face into the mess of her hair on the pillow and let her two fingers pull gentle lines across his cheek until he felt quiet enough to sleep.

הַנָּמֵר וְהַשּׁוֹחֵט

THE TIGER AND THE BUTCHER

§

Kislev, 5699

December 1938

As I watch Meyer, I can't help but watch his hands: quick, large, and surprisingly smooth, with the look of soft worn-in leather. They do not look like the hands of a man whose work is done with a cleaver, a man who deals with cold meat and blood. It is easy to picture him hauling those heavy slabs though, onto his butcher's block and wielding those heavy metal tools. When not cutting meat, he uses his hands mostly to talk with. During one particular performance, sitting with his legs kicked out in front of him, the grand sway of his paw almost caught my attentively-listening uncle on the cheek. When not speaking, which is not often, he keeps his imposing body perfectly still and cups his hands over his knees. In the days since our arrival when he greeted us at the inn, I have seen him only two ways: rambling and gesturing broadly, or silently holding his large knees in his even larger palms.

The *shochet*, Meyer Zalesky, has visited us in the evenings at the inn each day we've been here. We even sat with his family this morning at shul. It is hard to believe that more than one whole week has passed since

Uncle and I set out on our journey. While the number of days and the length of the distance may be short, I am aware of how very far away I am now from when we set off. This place is more like home: larger than the last stop because it is so close to Nowogrodek, a real city. The inn we're staying at is far fancier than I expected. *Shochet* Zalesky told me that the council had pulled out all the stops to welcome my uncle, his reputation having so much preceded him. Unsure of what Zalesky meant, I just smiled, happy to be equally benefiting from this show of hospitality.

It is my first time at an inn, and it is nicer than any home I've ever been in. The curtains are thick and black with an ivy pattern in raised copper velvet. Once they are shut the whole room warms up, even at night when Uncle and I have put out the fire. And then there is that — a small stove in every room! Our first night here, Uncle let me keep it going all night; I wanted to breathe in the smell of burning wood and coal as I was drifting to sleep. Even Uncle seemed to appreciate this little indulgence. Tonight, we'll have the first Chanukah candle to fall asleep by. The smell won't be quite the same, but I've never slept in the same room as the menorah before either. I imagine the light it will create, with the warm copper in the curtains, will be beautiful. The *shochet* has brought us a menorah from his family; we'll have dinner and light the candles at his home, but he thought we should have one in our room as well. I have never known anyone with two menorahs. Naturally, I could tell right away that he was a successful man. Not just any old butcher but also to hold the honoured distinction of being *shochet*, he walks and dresses like an important man. I am eager to see his home. I'm sure it's magnificent. The three of us will go together as soon as he finishes his story.

The Zalesky family consists of Meyer, his wife Tsippe, their daughter Rivkah, and all four grandparents who live with them in their large home. Meyer's parents are just as large as he is and just as fond of sitting. Tsippe and her parents are tiny. They flutter noiselessly in the home like little birds between Meyer and his oak-like parents. Rivkah is the perfect daughter of both. The sum of the adults that surround her, she has her father's imposing build and her mother's silent nature. She is my age and at least my height. At first I thought she was shy — an endearing quality in girls I think, and one that made me like her instantly. I was mistaken. She has been staring at me all through dinner. Wide, deep-set eyes set on my face the entire time. She is nothing like shy— merely bold and quiet. It makes me uneasy in my own skin. I find myself adjusting my hair, the collar of my shirt, brushing the strings of my tzitzit; very fidgety and immature and unlike me at all. I do not like being watched, especially when I eat. I wonder what kind of job Tsippe Zalesky has been doing, raising a daughter that doesn't seem to know how rude it is to stare.

We are having both brisket and chicken. Meyer is as excessive with his table as he is with the volume of his voice. "When a Jewish man has a chicken on his table it is because one of them is sick," Meyer's voice sends wet white fluffs of half-chewed food onto the tablecloth. "But not with such guests." The force of his laughter has Tsippe shiver in her chair, a willow caught in a sudden storm. He is too loud, too showy, and she is afraid of her own shadow.

"Tonight is a double celebration. That we should have company for the holidays," she suggests, no doubt to make up for her husband's brashness. My uncle blushes his response, and Tsippe looks pleased.

There is a hardness to Rivkah's silence. Her father speaks non-stop and everyone smiles or laughs politely, but Rivkah's face remains sullen and still. It is hard not to stare back at her though my gaze on her face appears to go unnoticed. The bridge of her nose is wide and only slightly rounded, a smooth small slope that is echoed in her cheeks and in the shape of her chin. There is something about her face that appears unlooked at. Unseen. Our eyes don't meet. She seems able to look around my eyes, to somehow take in my whole face at once, without focus. It is like looking into a picture: her face looks right back out at me but is frozen, unresponsive. I force myself to look away, concentrate on Meyer and his ever-changing, ever-moving facial expressions and open mouth.

Still, I can feel her gaze pressing on my skin, only breaking when her mother calls on her to help clear the table.

There are three large rooms that make up the main level of the house. The front door opens into a large kitchen behind which a wide staircase leads to the second floor. To the right of the kitchen is the dining room, with a long oak table and twelve high-backed chairs with upholstered seats. The walls are covered in dark grey wallpaper dotted with red and navy blossoms. The final room is the sitting area, which has several windows and two great mirrors that sit in heavy wooden frames. Every chair in this room is upholstered and again, there are twelve of them. All three rooms are approximately the same size, like in a precisely-made dollhouse. I must admit that I have never seen such a house. Softly lit, the whole sitting room glows like the inside of a gilded chandelier. In the corner is a piano. There is even a table lamp that sits above it, a light set aside solely to illuminate the keys.

After dinner, through the lighting of the first candle and conversation afterwards, I wait for Meyer to announce who in the household is so talented to play it. But it is never mentioned—never looked at. Usually Uncle would comment on such a lovely instrument, but even to him it is invisible, as if I were the only one in the room to notice it standing there.

Before it gets too late, Meyer offers to escort Uncle and me back to the inn. "Very kind offer but you're already home. Besides, Yitzhak and I always enjoy an evening walk."

———

There is a low breeze, which glides along the street and freezes my calves. The rest of the air is perfectly motionless around us, most of the houses dark except for a flash of candlelight in their windows. We walk on the bank of the street, moving quickly and kicking up snow which lands back down on the top of our shoes like momentary blankets that keep our feet from suffering the way our legs do.

"You can see, can't you, that sometimes even the most important men, even ones who might hold righteous positions in the community, can have misplaced values." Uncle speaks and then blows into his cupped hands, puffs of steam sneaking through his loosely laced fingers. "He recites fables and proverbs but doesn't understand their meaning." More hot air hits the night and Uncle clasps his hands tightly together before moving them to his pockets. "It is not about gross adornment or sparse piety. No one man needs have so much when so many must get by with so little. A man who knows the true value of things would recognize that this is not a time of prosperity — even if it is for just himself, it is not for his community, which should count for as much." I realize that Uncle had not blushed at Tsippe's spread to be polite but rather in embarrassment for all that had been wasted in his honour. Too much food in too large a home.

———

The large shul stretches for an entire block at the centre of the shtetl and is at least a street-length wide. The sanctuary is shaped unlike any other shul I have ever seen, in a half circle. Its back wall stretches the length of the building and is covered in large cabinets, each at least the width of my arms reached out side to side. The cabinet doors are thick wood with brass frames that reach beyond the height of the doors to the base of the second floor balcony that serves as the women's gallery. Inside these cabinets are several *genizot* and areas of special storage for Torah covers and prayer books. Behind the first door I opened were piles of old books stacked together with their faded and ripped spines showing, bits of string dangling between dusty covers.

The bimah is at the centre of the semi-circle, itself curved like a half moon. Behind it are three rectangular stained-glass windows, spraying the bimah with colours of light. The first, in shades of blue, depicts the intended sacrifice of Abraham's son Isaac. The middle window shows the parting of the Red Sea in different shades of red. The story in the third window, painted in tones of green, is the hardest to recognize. Uncle explains to me that it is the world when it was wiped clean by the flood. There is no ark, but the waves of green are clear and full, they emanate from a ripple caused by the wings of a small dove in the corner of the glass, upon whose back is draped an olive branch.

It will take Uncle and me much longer to get our task done here, but at least this time we have such a majestic room to do it in — not on our knees on the floor amidst piles of rubble. Not in a small, cramped room with only a sliver of a window for light. During our time sorting papers, Uncle gets so deep in concentration that rather than breaking for lunch, he merely sends me for our food and I bring it back for him. We eat in the council's office, one of the rooms that fill up the building's space that has been cut-out by the sanctuary.

As a member of the welcoming committee and someone very proud of having spare food, it was Meyer Zalesky who volunteered his wife to prepare our meals. The first time I went, I rushed myself all the way there and all the way back. Uncle hadn't seemed to notice I had been gone at all. The next day was colder, and I couldn't help but be slowed down. I felt my arms and legs freezing as I walked, and Tsippe insisted I warm up some before she'd let me leave again. Uncle still didn't notice. He sits surrounded by overwhelming volumes of books and community ledgers.

It takes longer for him to decide what should be done with each item, so I spent most of those first few days watching him read and letting my mind wander. It was boring, and I sensed Uncle becoming agitated with my just sitting there, having nothing to look at but his face buried deep in papers. Now I take as long as I can getting our lunches, discovering new routes between the shul and the Zalesky home, looking in shops on the way or watching the younger boys on the skating rink they've made outside the market. At first I didn't like having to go in and spending time in the Zalesky home, Tsippe pushing me towards the stove to warm up, but now I go straight in without her insisting. It's been several days, and I am used to these visits.

No one seems to notice all the time Rivkah and I spend alone together. I am noticed and acknowledged each time I arrive at the Zalesky home, but Tsippe is soon re-absorbed in her chores, always moving quickly in and out of rooms, always in motion. She has two girls from the neighbourhood who she pays to help around the house. They talk to each other but never to me. Her mother and mother-in-law have, after my first few visits, lost interest in my being there, so I am left in Rivkah's company.

At first, we would just sit in front of the windows together and not speak, but I detest uneasy silence, so I started to tell her about Ben and Sarah, Mama and Papa. Then I told her a little about Pietka (as much as I thought she was mature enough to know and where Uncle and I are headed next. It is exhausting doing all the talking, and I can never tell if she is listening.

"You don't help your mother around the house. Why

not?" A direct question, I'll force her to speak. She can certainly outlast me when it comes to keeping silent but not to answer a question would be just rude, and I wouldn't stand for it. Rivkah turns and looks right at me. Her face has the same emptiness, her eyes a focus somewhere beyond me. With my hands on my hips, I shift in my seat, letting her know I'm prepared to leave if she insists on keeping this up.

"We've always had help. I do my share, but Mama prefers it this way." Rivkah does not look down or away when she speaks, her eyes make no hint or reflection of what she has said. "It's always been that way. Papa insists." A part of me is relieved at not having to get up and leave...not just yet. It's cold and I have nowhere else to go except back to the shul where I will only be in the way. She is still looking at me. I realize I had not expected so short an answer, but here I am with her waiting for me to say something else or ask again. In my mind, I sift through traces of polite conversation: simple, easy questions I could ask or would ask anyone.

"Do you ever get to go into Nowogrodek? I hear they have a very large market." Rivkah blinks but does not respond; her face waits for more, something else. "Do you play the piano?"

The slopes of her face redden, not to a blush but like winter hands in front of a fire, "No."

"My sister Sarah and I both play the flute." Again, a blink but no reply. Still flush, she raises her elbow so it

92

rests on the arm of her chair and her body is turned toward me. My ears pulse hot with frustration; she can insist on saying nothing, but I won't let it go. I return my gaze to the window and slip the words out under my breath, more annoyed than even I expected. "Why do you even have a piano?"

"My sister plays." I am now so aware of her eyes on me that I can feel them, even without turning, leave my face. I know where she is looking; I know without turning my head but do it anyways to stare at her, surprised. And just like before, she seems not to notice my staring at her, does not respond to my shock in any way, her face still a blank slate. The moist skin on her palms squeaks over the polished wood of the chair's arms as she clutches them tightly in each hand. For the first time, unbidden, Rivkah continues to speak.

———

For a week when I was seven years old, my mother left the house every morning in her black dress and shawl and did not return until dinnertime. Sarah took care of Ben and me, watched the house and did the cooking. She didn't tell me anything about where Mama was going except that the Gorshmans had suffered a great tragedy. Faige Gorshman was a woman my mother had grown up with; I spent a lot of time at their house, playing with their four children. I was old enough to know from the way she was dressed and the way she was acting that

Mama was visiting a shivah house, but until Sarah said Faige's name, I didn't know whose. I begged her to tell me what happened but all she said was it was a great tragedy and Mama didn't want to talk about it so I shouldn't ask.

And I never did. I even resisted the temptation to try to listen to what Mama and Papa were talking about at night. Mainly because I could tell she was crying. But now there were only three Gorshman children, and soon everyone, even seven-year-olds, knew what had happened.

A couple of years ago Shira, their oldest and a friend of Sarah's, got married. It was a perfect wedding; everyone was happy, and everyone was there. Even Faige and her husband looked happier than I had seen them in years. The next day, though, Mama left early again, and this time didn't return until long after the sun had set. I could tell she had been to visit her friend. I could tell they had both been crying and talking about Faige's lost daughter, Leah. She had devastated her family by going off with a young man who was not Jewish. He wasn't even Polish but an immigrant from Yugoslavia. Mama was crying because her friend had lost a daughter and any future grandchildren, and she mourned them both. Even a mitzvah like a daughter's wedding stung Faige with the memory of her loss. Sarah said that Mama cried for and with Faige, since she was a mother herself.

Leah Gorshman had been sixteen; Ida Zalesky had been eighteen.

———

I had a dream last night. It was familiar, something I have dreamt before but not for a long time. When I was little it had been a nightmare and even last night, it woke me out of a heavy sleep. Years ago, it was something I had pictured during the day or, at least, tried to picture, but it was never frightening. But when I saw it at night, I always woke up in a panic.

No one in our household has ever died. I have travelled for family funerals, seen burials, seen others sit shivah; my parents' parents died before I was born, but I watched my father sit for his brothers. Still, I had never been there that first day when the *chevra kadisha* arrived to prepare the body. The men with their candles, mirrors being covered, arrangements being made. I was seven and I would struggle to imagine a room full of family with upset, mournful faces. And candles, dozens and dozens of them lit and flickering in a room where the air refused to move. So many candles that the people were careful to hold their breath so as not to blow any out. Candles laid out around an invisible body, an absent body. Leah's body.

It is meant to be simple: live, die, bury. But what if there is no body? With a regular ghost, the body dies, and the spirit goes on. Here the person, the spirit, is dead but the body is still out there somewhere. A ghost turned inside out. When I woke last night, it was not fear that sat with me, lingering long after I was fully awake, long after Uncle's leaden body in the wide bed beside me in our room at the inn had reassured me of where I was and that I was not alone. It was something weightier, an ill ease. I felt homesick and I couldn't shake it, nor could I get back to sleep.

———

"Why didn't you ever learn to play?"

Rivkah is wearing her light blonde hair in a long braid that hangs down her back, spilling out of her yellow babushka. Today we match; my thick wool sweater is lemon-coloured. We are the perfect pair. Sitting on the piano's bench for the first time, I notice the dirt that has accumulated in between the black and white keys. No one has ever bothered to close the piano's lid, and the only way to reach the dirt with a rag would be to press down on the keys and to play one note at a time. Rivkah had been sitting near the windows when I arrived, but as soon as I came in, she led us both to the piano. She has been silent, as usual. Each day, I have come and tried every different topic of discussion I can think of: music, family, my trip, her father's business, even the size of her house. Nothing can make her speak. She answers only about her sister and even then, her voice is quiet, and the words clipped, worried that someone might hear. I repeat my question, "Why didn't you learn?"

Rivkah shrugs, "I was never good at it. Soon after she left, my parents stopped my lessons. It's out of tune now, I think. I could never tell."

"We leave in a few days, my uncle and I. I think we're heading north towards Vilna next. I'm not sure. We don't have a definite route."

"She was naturally good at piano. Like Papa. Fast hands but without his fat fingers. I drew while she practiced. She would play; I would draw. And then we'd take walks. Always the two of us together. Papa promised her that when she got married, he would buy her a piano just like this one for her home."

"I should have brought along my wooden flute. I know it would have been a hassle to carry along and could be easily lost but I worry how out of practice I will be when I finally return home. I was quite good, a natural too. My papa says it makes sense because of how well I concentrate. I'm mainly very good at playing music."

Rivkah doesn't respond. She doesn't look like she has heard me anyway. Her face is gone again, lost, turned towards me but in that empty blank way. It's enough that I have finally gotten used to her glaring, but I cannot get over her disinterest. She does not know how to hold a polite conversation. For the hundredth time during this visit, I contemplate leaving and heading back to the shul where at least I could talk to someone of some interest. The pedal is stiff under the pressure of my boot, but I keep pushing anyways. I cannot explain why but its stubbornness infuriates me. I push down so hard that my toes buckle over themselves with the pressure and my sock begins to bunch towards the front of my boot. Rivkah leans back on the bench and peers below the level of the keys, watching my struggle. With my right foot on top of my left one now, I work their increased weight back and forth on the brassy metal spoon. Finally, it shifts, and the wooden instrument exhales a low exhausted sound, *thwump,* as the metal gives against velvet and the strings bow. Rivkah exhales, too, and there is another sound, which is hers. Deep and low like the piano. My feet slide off the petal and it settles again into its mute position.

Rivkah looks at me, for the first time right at me, "Can I give you something?"

––––––

It is my last day here and I make excuses to Uncle about why I will not go to the Zalesky's today and visit as usual. I cannot go, but it would do no good to try to explain; if he knew what Rivkah had given me he would be furious. It is a trespass of some kind, I'm sure of it. And a lie. To agree to carry something: to pretend that I will keep a look out and attempt to deliver the undeliverable. I couldn't say no to her, as she wanted me to take it so badly. Buying lunch today from the baker's, just a cold roll with butter each instead of the hot meal Tsippe must surely have prepared for us, I fondle the folded papers in my vest coat pocket.

I had the dream again, about Leah Gorshman or about Ida Zalesky, I cannot be sure. They are both dead, and I would rather not bump into either of them, let alone go looking for their resemblance in the face of every new person I meet.

Rivkah could not bear to part with the only picture she had of her sister. She said it was the only picture she was able to save from her father's rampage. She said he tore the house into shreds: everywhere, in the centre of the floor of each room, any reminder of Ida was de-stroyed—torn up by him and tossed to the ground, little pieces flying out from his strong butcher's hands. Rivkah described the scene, and I did my best to picture it. It was not what I had witnessed, not Mama's sadness nor Faige Gorshman's distant grief.

I pictured faces of a girl, the same face at different ages—three, ten, fourteen, eighteen—disappearing into his two large hands, the skin worn smooth from a lifetime of use. Then, the face reappears bit by bit — a nose, the same nose only younger and older, the eyes, an eyebrow, the hem of a dress — and falls into piles of Ida on the floor...Ida at every age. Rivkah could not bear to part with her one picture, so she sketched Ida's face from the photo onto a piece of paper, which she wrapped around her letter's envelope. It was tied into place with two thick pieces of string, one at either end so that Ida's face was not hidden at all. Instead, the girl's pencilled face was framed by the white spun cotton. Very thin, Ida has none of her sister's face with its slopes and curves. Where on Rivkah there is fullness, Ida appears hollow – a severe dip, lovingly shaded, splits her upper lip in two.

"I do not know her name now," Rivkah's voice was uneven when she had handed me the letter. "I think she might have changed it...she must have. Her last name, at least, of course. But she'll look the same. She always did. Like Mama. So you'll see her and recognize her and won't forget." She said she had begun thinking about giving me the sketch of her sister the day she met me, the night we came to dinner but had been, until just then, unsure of whether or not she could trust me. I said she could. I promised her that I would do my best and she could trust me entirely.

I lied.

The weight of her letter on me is my every second thought. It deserves to be seen. If that is true, then this feeling guilty is nonsense. And it is true that words on a paper are of no use to Ida anymore; they cannot reach her anyways. I wait until I am in the alley behind the bakery to slide it open. I have to close my eyes while I rip the envelope's carefully glued seal. The tearing paper is loud in my ears and the whiteness of the page in between Rivkah's perfect black letters is unexpected; it forces my

eyes to slide quickly over her words — there is too much
to take in.

*Sister ... this letter has had one million drafts, perhaps
one a day since you left, written in my head, kept there.
I erase bits, replace them with others, change words
and move them around... I address you differently each
time: sister, dear sister, Ida, Ida, Ida. I like the sound of
your name in my head. I haven't spoken it for so long...
the sound is staler spoken aloud, as if my mouth forming
the words is out of tune and out of practice. Inside it is
still smooth and warm, still full of you...*

*No one is the same and yet nothing has changed. It
is as if Mama and Papa have become more of who they
always were... he is even louder, it started soon after.
Using his voice to fill the room and take up the new
empty spaces created by Mama's silence. She is even
less talkative now... her laughter sounds fake, there to
make him happy... I mourn my loss of you more than I
ever could their slipping away...*

*... it will be my turn soon though no one speaks of
it to me. They talk of boys my age when I'm not in the
room. I hear them, though, just as we have always heard
everything that was not meant for us. I feel bad I want
marriage so little, but I know it will be better for them
after I've left... I think there will be very few things I
will miss. Your piano, maybe, and my room... I still took
lessons for a little while after you were gone but I was*

miserable at it and it put Papa in the worst moods. So one day the teacher just stopped coming and we all pretended like nothing had happened...

Every morning I check but still I look nothing like you. I think Mama is disappointed... The girls still come to help but now I do some of the ironing. I'd rather be in the back doing that with Bubbe than in the kitchen. Mama never asks me to do it but it gets me out of the way so I take it without asking...

The mornings are still my favourite time of day...

I wonder about his family. If they can be at all like ours was? If they did to him what was done to you? If you've met them, if he looks like his father... Do you speak with them? ... I do not want to fill your letter with questions. I will never get answers; it doesn't seem fair. I picture you, all the time, him too. I imagine him as everything you explained him to be... I can't see where you're living. It is so hard to imagine some things: your house, your clothes... I hope there is at least one room big enough for you... I picture the weather a lot, where you are. At least I know the weather; you'd have to go very far away for that to change much. I like knowing that when it snows here it is likely snowing there and the sun rises at the same time for you...

It's Chanukah. Is it Chanukah for you? Does he let you light the menorah or do you even want to? I try to picture your face but I am scared it may have changed. We cannot be the same people in two different lives.

When you left, I cried because if what they said was true, we wouldn't be going to the same heaven. I'm old enough to know better now...

I would give it all up for you... I would give them away... I am dead too, I think...

If I have to let go of everything else, the entire world, I will not let go of you... your sister, R.

§

It took Jake almost three weeks to track down the pamphlet. He'd spent over three decades moving through the city, but it was only in those past few days that he had ever really noticed how many monuments there were, for this war and others: names inscribed into marble, into stone, lists a hundred names long. But none of them matched the paper in the folder—a ripped page from a pamphlet with one family under-lined and the name of a girl meticulously circled. *Rivkah.* It should have been a dead end, like so many of the others, but Jake wasn't ready to give up on this one. More than a name in a list, this name was on something real...something he could hold in his hands. Jake knew someone had to have put her name on the list for the memorial. Maybe that someone was Ike, and Jake had to know. He felt sure. He had to know.

Each day he called another synagogue, another organiza-tion, and visited another memorial site. Every name his eyes passed over felt familiar. After finding nothing, he would leave, but the sounds of them would stay with him. Walking to the metro, or in his car, the rhythm of it he would play over and over in his head: *Zalkind, Zedner, Zleiman, Zlater, Zundell.* It was a woman at the Genealogical Society who suggested he check the Musée de l'Holocauste Montréal. It had been on his list, but he hadn't gotten to it yet.

"Yup, that seems like it was one of ours." The docent was a boy who looked barely old enough to be out of high school. "I can't be sure if it's still part of the permanent exhibitions, but I can get you someone who'd know." It took a moment for Jake to register what the kid had said. "If you want to go look at our Ancestry display, I'll have them find you there." He put a map of the museum in Jake's hand and disappeared. Jake flinched; he needed a moment to get his bearings. He unfolded the map and scanned the page for the Ancestry exhibit. It was not far from where he stood at the information desk and would not be hard to find at all, but Jake traced the path with his finger several times before moving.

———

The pamphlet was from a Yom Hashoah ceremony in 1989: ten years after the museum opened. Names were put on banners that had been hung all around the museum and also inscribed in the pamphlets handed out to the crowd. Shanye, the woman from the Holocaust Centre attached to the museum, told Jake there had been an impressive attendance that year. "Some years more, some years less. But 1989, it was an anniversary of sorts." Jake told Shanye why he had come. He needed to know if his father had put the names on the list. Despite himself, Jake told her everything: about his father's death, the trip in 1938, his search to find the people on the list. He was getting used to spreading these new details after so many years of brushing questions off by being just a "survivor's son." They were the layers of a story he was learning how to tell, including when to pause, the rhythm of it all now familiar and, at times, easy.

Shanye, attractive and tanned in her late fifties, held a hand on her chest while he spoke. Her mauve painted nails clutched and pulled on a silver pendant which hung from her neck. "Well, of course, we keep all those records at the centre. Let me just go downstairs and check. It might take a while. There's a cafeteria, I can meet you there if you want to wait." He did. So she left him standing in front of a frosted glass tableau: Montreal Holocaust Survivors/Descendants.

Over an hour later, Shanye found Jake on a bench in the bright white and grey cafeteria and gave him what he had come for: a name. Without reading it, he tucked the papers she handed him into his pocket. Jake thanked her and got up to leave.

"Before you go, would you consider writing your father's story down? It would be such a worthwhile addition to our Kristallnacht exhibition."

Jake hesitated. "Maybe I'll come back."

Shanye nodded and held out her hand. "You just let me know. If you feel like putting it down."

Sitting in the driver's seat of his car, Jake pulled the papers out of his coat pocket: three photocopied pages stapled together, and folded inside that, a fresh copy of the Yom Hashoah pamphlet. The first copied page was a letter explaining the purpose behind the 1989 exhibit. Jake flipped it quickly over without reading it. The second page was the information sheet, but the name on it was not his father's. He let his eyes fall over the rest of the page, running across ink that cluttered the white space. No Ike, no Isaac, nothing. Indeed, the handwriting was not his father's, either. The script was graceful, the looped arms of the l's and d's posed like ballerinas. Disappointed, Jake re-read the name of the woman who had filled out the sheets and posted the names: Ida Plaski, followed by an address only. Jake glanced quickly at the third page, a form with the letterhead of the museum, surprisingly familiar, and tucked it inside his coat pocket. He had one more stop to make before going home.

———————

"So you're going to Quebec City?" Seda picked up the thin pile of papers which sat in front of Jake and began flipping through them.

"Yeah, I figure it's only a day's drive there and back."

"Good. I think you should. What year was this?"

"1989. I was sixteen. I got into a car accident." Jake was surprised he said it and surprised he made the connection. "I'd never been in so much trouble in my life. I think my dad

106

was extra mad because it meant he had to actually try to parent me instead of just waiting for me to, I don't know, come to fruition."

She gave him a sleepy sort of smile and looked back at the papers in her hands. "Your dad was there, huh." Seda was comparing Ike's pamphlet scrap with the copy Shanye had provided.

"Hadn't thought about it," he lied. "Guess so, he must have been. The lady said they handed them out at the service." Jake sat at the table across from her. The kitchen in the apartment they shared was small; the table only sat four and was just barely compact enough to fit in the corner. They had taken the apartment for the exposed brick which lined one side of the entire space. That and the fireplace. It didn't work, but Seda swore it still smelled like burning wood. A phantom smell.

Seda pursed her lips and flipped the page. There must have been hundreds and hundreds of names and not at all in alphabetical order. Rather, the pamphlet was organized to resemble the way the names had been put together on the banners. Seda dragged a much-chewed pen along the lines so as not to lose her place. "That's what I thought," she said, flipping the pen around and drawing a star in the margin. She held the marked page out towards him, tilting her head and watching his face. He had suspected, a part of him had at least, but then why wouldn't his father have kept the whole thing? Why keep the underlined name of a stranger's family and not your own? Jake hadn't wanted to look, but there they were:

Lillian and Mordechai. Benjamin and Sarah. And great uncle Yakov. He would ask Zalman on their next call.

————

For the last two years, Ike had been even slower to get anywhere, having to leave for everything extra early or risk being late. It drove the teenaged Jake crazy, but Ike was resolute. He would never take the expressway again since the flood. All those people trapped and the water rising. "It came out of nowhere," he would say when Jake pressed. "The rain came without warning."

And so, of course, when he got his license and took the car out for an inaugural drive, he hadn't hesitated. He merged onto Décarie, heading into downtown. And of course, there had been construction, blocked lanes, a series of road signs and closed exits that everyone seemed to know instinctively but him. How could he? He was never on this road. When it happened, when he heard the metallic crunch of his father's bumper against the car ahead of him, he knew right away Ike would be even angrier because of where it had happened.

That night, Jake had answered after dinner when Zalman called. He mumbled something about being grounded and passed the receiver over to his father before heading upstairs to start his sentence.

"I yelled at him," Ike said, hearing footsteps reach the hallway upstairs.

"Good. Fathers can yell."

"He makes everything about her, you know. 'You don't know what it's like, you don't know what it's like.' He tells me over and over. What he doesn't know..." Ike's voice and thoughts trail off.

"What he doesn't know you don't say. He lost her too."

"Pfft. I don't like the word in English. 'Lost.' I didn't lose my wife, Zeama. Jacob didn't lose his mother. I know exactly where she is. She's in the ground. I just can't get to her."

"You think your father needed a piece of paper to remember their names?"

Jake could hear the sound of dogs whining in the background over the phone. And then Zalman's voice, muffled shouting, "*Arop, arop. Gut. Esn,*" followed by the sound of kibble being poured into a plastic dish. Zalman returned his voice to the mouthpiece. "You know, your mother is in there, too. Rojina." The word brought with it a memory which stung the back of Jake's eyelids. Only two people ever called his mother that: this man and the one she'd married. It was the shock at his own reaction which kept tears from sprouting in the corners of his eyes. "Not her, but her family. Your father would never forget."

Jake played with the phone cord wrapped around his finger. "But you have no idea who this Ida is then?"

"No, no. I only met your father later. I only know how it all ended." A February breeze pressed a wayward leaf against

Zalman's window. He knocked on the glass to set it back into flight. "You should do it, I'm thinking. What the woman said."

"What woman?" Jake stared at Ida's name on the page in front of him.

"Write it down. Write the whole of everything down and to give it to them."

Jake had only mentioned Shanye and her request in passing, the blank form still tucked inside his jacket. "It's not really important right now."

Zalman dropped his head and shook it as if Jake could see. "It is. Now it is," he thrust his hands in front of him, pushing the evening air. "Do it. It would be a good thing."

Jake felt his voice stiffen, every syllable bristling at the urgency in Zalman's tone. "Well, he was there. It's his story. I barely know what happened let alone any of the details. If that would have been such a good thing, why didn't he do it? Why didn't he write what happened down? Or even, just…" Jake squeezed his eyes shut and let his shoulders drop heavily forward, slumping deep in his chair.

On the other side of the Atlantic, Zalman held the phone with both hands, cradling the smooth plastic to his cheek. He wanted to explain, but he only had guesses himself.

Jake counted his breaths, pushing in and out, out of him, into the receiver. He counted their echo in his ear. Zalman heard them, too, and though he could not be seen and said nothing, began nodding his head as if to reassure them both. Nodding, he waited.

"I'm afraid the more I look for him, the more..." Jake's hand landed on his lap, letting go of the phone cord.

It had gotten dark in both men's cities. The late afternoon sky in Montreal was squeezing out the last corners of sunshine, while thousands of miles away, Zalman's tropical air was loosening its grip on the pink and orange shadow of a sun already set. It was late and enough had been said. Tomorrow Jake would drive to Quebec City, uninvited, and hope the unknown woman was home. Hope she would be as eager to talk to him as he would be to speak with her. He needed to get off the phone, get organized, and try to get some sleep. Zalman would be up for hours. At his age, he didn't sleep much anymore.

"I'm afraid the more I look for him, the more I'll lose him. The more I realize I didn't know, the less I ever had."

———————

The eyes that met him at the door were a dark enough brown as to be almost black. Startled, expecting a woman at least sixty years older, Jake tripped over his words: "Hi, hello. I'm looking for a Mrs. Ida Plaski. My name is Jake Langley."

The woman looked Jake up and down and then leaned out the doorway to examine his slush-covered car in the driveway. "Is my grandmother expecting you?"

"Oh, no. I'm afraid I just thought I'd stop by." He realized he would have to explain himself further. She was opening her mouth, no doubt to get rid of him, when he interrupted, "I think she was a friend of my father's. I was hoping I would be able to talk to her."

"What is this about?"

"I really...if I could just speak with your grandmother."

"One second." The woman, with light brown hair that fell pin straight and tucked behind her ears, held the door between her two hands and turned her back on him and the cold air outside. "Momma?" A chair scraped against a tile floor somewhere inside. "I'll just go see."

The door closed. He kicked his boot against the railing to beat off the caked-on snow and mud. He had gotten out of the car at least three times on the relatively short trip to clean his back windshield and side view mirrors, the wet dirt and soot having flown up from his own tires and those of passing trucks constantly impairing his view, making for a miserably slow-going drive.

The doorframe of the house in front of which he stood was painted beige to match the siding. In fact, the whole neighbourhood was made up of houses painted varying shades of dull or dreary. There was no sign, neither on the house nor on the face of the woman who had answered the door, that he had come to the right place. Indeed, Jake was overwhelmed by the feeling that he was somehow out of place. But the name was her grandmother's. He would find something there.

"I'm sorry. I don't think now is a very good time." Jake hadn't noticed the crack in the door open. It was the grand-daughter again, only her face exposed to the outside air. About halfway down the length of the door Jake saw another face, a young girl whose hair matched her mother's, peering up at him. Ida's great-granddaughter was trying to get outside but was being held back by her mother's tight grip on the collar of her shirt.

"Please, it's very important." Jake dug his hand into the pocket of his coat and pulled out the torn piece of pamphlet with the Zalesky family circled on it. He held the paper out towards her, but the woman didn't move. "It was my father's." A six-year-old hand reached up and took the paper from him, her little face disappearing from the doorway. The woman sighed and again Jake was left facing the outside of a closed door.

It took a few minutes, but eventually Jake was let inside. The little girl, who introduced herself as Becca before her mother could prevent her, took his coat and disappeared with it into one of the rooms off the foyer. "I'm Leba. My grandmother's in the kitchen cooking. You can come in there." Jake followed the woman into the house and was seated at the kitchen table. Ida sat across from him looking down, her hands smoothing the pamphlet scrap on the tabletop. Her hair, dyed almost platinum blonde, was thin and teased enough to see through to her scalp. She must have been almost ninety. A pair of bifocals hung from a loop around her neck. Beneath that, she wore a delicate gold cross on a chain that sat resting on the table when she bent over. Unsure of himself, Jake waited for her to look at him before saying anything. In the meantime, he watched her hands moving over and over again across the paper. They were shaking. When she did look up, Jake noticed that her shoulders, too, were unsteady. "Where did you get this?"

"It was my father's, Isaac Langley. I'm his son, Jacob." He thought twice before stretching his hand out towards hers.

"Where, then, did he get it?" The skin on her face was thin, hanging loose but smooth around her eyes and over her high cheekbones. Every feature was delicate, small, draped elegantly in skin which had the texture of wet paper, shiny, soft. Jake told her about how he had gotten her name and information from the Museum. "The pamphlet is from the Yom Hashoah service. But you know that."

"Of course." Ida held the paper in her hands while she spoke, while she listened. On the other side of the room, her granddaughter watched them intensely, arranging clean chopped vegetables into a large wooden bowl. Jake could feel both of their eyes on him, one from in front and one from behind.

"I figured, well, my father kept things that were important to him and since the name on the pamphlet was circled..."

"My sister." Ida interrupted; looking down at the paper again she pointed at "Rivkah."

"Oh," Jake's mounting anxiety raised his back high up in his seat, "then you knew my father?"

Ida clicked her tongue against the back of her front teeth and shook her head. "No."

"No?" They both stared at the scrap in her hands until Ida wrapped her fingers around the paper. She gripped her fist, the knuckles bared through her skin, twitching with her effort.

She was clutching so tight it seemed that any moment the ink, though decades old, would be squeezed out and run dripping from between her fingers.

"How did your father know my sister?"

Jake broke into the now well-worn description of his particular quest: his father's death, the folder among all the other papers, names, places, dates. The words tumbled out of him in a mess upon the table. A trip through Poland, a separate mission, through towns, many little towns, maybe her town. He stopped and retraced his words, going over them again in his mind, wondering if he'd missed something. In the midst of his rambling, Ida's granddaughter had darted out of the kitchen in response to a loud thud from the other room.

The two of them momentarily alone, Jake searched the woman's face. He was expecting some sign of the recognition that he had found in Chaim. "So, I know it was a very long time ago and maybe not something you think about often but that must have been where you met him. How he knew your family."

Ida ran her empty hand through a curl of hair and set it down, a fist on the table in front of her. "1938. I was not there." She rubbed her fists in circles on the table and Jake, despite himself, held his breath full and expectant inside his lungs. "I never knew your father."

Jake exhaled, deeply. She had nothing to tell him that he could not stand to hear. Nothing he could not stand to know. The shiny old woman mistook his new posture for simple disappointment. She lay her hand flat out on the table in front of him and tapped it gently. There was a new softness in her voice which echoed itself in the folds of her face. "My granddaughter can make us something to drink."

They sat at the kitchen table and talked while Ida's granddaughter served them coffee and finished making dinner. When she was done, she sat at the table beside her grandmother, clutching the old woman's hand in her lap. At some point, the young girl had crawled into the room. The only sign of her was the sound of shuffling on the floor and the clunk of a tiny foot in a tiny shoe hitting one of the table legs. She sat quietly beneath them, all the while with one arm slung around her mother's leg and the other playing with the laces on her great-grandmother's tan shoes.

Ida held Jake with her eyes while she spoke, "I should have seen some of that in your face when you came here. That you were an orphan." She blinked and an almost tear lost its grip, dampening the skin under her eye. "Like me."

"I was so unsure then. And if I had known," she shook an unhappy finger at him, "that someone could just go and find me I might not have. But my Rivkah, I miss her so much." The three of them stared at the girl's name on the crinkled page. Underlined, circled in black ink. Ida returned her lenses to the bridge of her nose and turned the paper so that the letters stood upright before her. "Your father must have known her well." Ida smiled at Jake, "She was easy to love. She was the one who was easy to love."

It was time, he decided. Without the burden of fear that came with tales told of his own father, Jake gave into the nagging desire to ask, to know. It was what he needed, a story, her story, so as not to leave empty-handed. Ida's granddaughter kept one arm folded across her chest and the other on her grandmother. She would rush him out of there as soon as she could, whether worried that he had upset Ida or that dinner would get cold, Jake wasn't sure. "What happened to you? Then." The question came and went easily, as six-year-old fingers began to playfully tug on his pant leg.

Something changes inside of a person when they are certain they have nothing to lose. Nothing left—nothing else. It either deadens or quickens the spirit. But as long as they are alive, still feeling, still breathing, there is always more left to lose. More that can be taken away. It is an unfortunate truth that Ida Plaski, née Zalesky, knew more intimately than most. Ida told Jake that she had done "that typical girlish thing" and chosen a boy and what she could only describe as love over her entire world. "He was my *bashert*. It might have been puppy love but what did I know. I was a puppy. Both so young then, a teenaged girl. He worked in the city, and we did not even know how to talk to each other. But we learned. He taught me Polish, and I learned how to be his wife." She ran off and married a man her family could never approve of. "Could not have, Jacob. They had no choice, and so I thought I had none either."

They had planned to go to Siberia but went to see his family along the Soviet border first. A Slavic boy married to a Jewish girl. "We were not welcome there, but we stayed. It was what he knew, and I thought already we had both given up so much. I could take the cold looks and shoulders — we were happy enough, us two." But armies move without regard for anyone's happiness. Ida had no papers; she'd destroyed them. Her conversion was never official. She was a woman with no shadow, no past to cast behind her—a ghost. What she did have was a new name, a fine Slavic name, and a new religion, and that was enough. "I spoke with a terrible accent. It didn't matter. A soldier with a gun does not bother much to hear what a shy girl has to say. I was not expected much to speak. Only answer to strangers yes and no."

The Russians had less hate for Slavs than for Jews, but not much less. Her husband was taken for five years as a labourer in one of the working gulags. And so they made it, finally and sadly, to Siberia. Separated, but alive. "He should have died in the forests of Katyn. I was sure he was dead. I thought I could feel it. I felt so much of that then. It was hard to tell whose death was in the air. We were all widows. All the wives knew, settled in a prison of our own, but..." Ida indulged in a painful smile. "He was not. He was moved. No one special, he was moved and almost seven years later, he was back to me." The army moved on and her husband found her, again, like he had the first time.

"From Siberia, his cousin helped us get to Canada."

"After the war?"

Afloat in the world of her own re-telling, Ida shook her head, "Years, years later. Almost 1960. Here there were jobs for men like my Sagan.

"I tried for years to find my sister. Like everyone else, I went to Red Cross, sent letters. But it was so much, there were so many people looking and so little of people to be found. When we got here, I looked again. And I finally found her."

It is what it means to have lost, what it is to survive. A lifetime spent searching for the dead in the face of every stranger you meet.

Jake remembered the title of the section which held her family's name in the pamphlet. A gravesite without head-stones, ashes rather than rows. "She died with our parents. I have nothing like a date but I do *yahrzteit* every year. On Yom Hashoah, 'day of remembrance,' so I remember."

A head sprouting from her lap teased Ida out of her nostalgia. Her great-granddaughter was thirsty and the time for dinner had come. The rest of the family would be home soon. It wouldn't be the same.

"I should probably let you get back to your evening." Jake smiled at them both. "I've already imposed too much."

Ida's granddaughter moved in her chair, ready to rise and walk him out, but was halted by the old woman's hand on her shoulder. Saying nothing, Ida led Jake out of the room, her granddaughter Leba static, frozen between sitting and standing in her seat.

Ida walked with Jake to the front door. Looking around the empty foyer, Jake remembered. "My coat. Becca took it."

She raised a finger to her lip to hush him and, taking his hand, guided him to the low landing of the L-shaped staircase which faced the door. Jake let himself be pulled down beside her. "I am a widow almost twenty years." The knuckles of her fingers which she held out in front of his face were curved, her "two" hunched before him. "Sagan is gone already eleven years. And I was a widow already before. Seven years while he was gone but more still when he came back."

The old woman shrugged, folding her hands on her knees. Her body was hot beside his, the smell of cooking clinging to every part of her. Her skin, her hair, the wool in her sweater and skirt. Now that he was so close to her, and now that they were alone again. "It takes time. I have thirteen grandchildren and even great grandchildren. Becca child is my youngest, but I have more. It can balance. I have three Rivkahs now. A daughter and granddaughters. We," she leaned close into him then, a secret's distance, "have enough dead to go around maybe, but I wanted her back."

He bit his lip, not quite understanding. Worried that the intrusion of his voice would sever this intimacy, Jake held both his tongue and his breath.

Her fingers flitted on the scoop of her collarbone, pressing the gold cross into her skin. "This is on the outside. I never take off. This is my husband, my children. It saved me." Letting go, her fingers slide over her heart. Jake follows the path they trace, tapping against her rib cage. "But this doesn't change. It's where she is." Before the last sound of the last word was fully his, Ida pulled away.

Walking away from him, she called into the kitchen before her, "Leba, his coat please." The two of them, Ida and her granddaughter, slid past each other in the kitchen doorway. The woman eyed her grandmother with concern but let her pass. Hurriedly, she disappeared into the other room and re-emerged with Jake's jacket, slightly rumpled, slung over her crossed arms. Jake watched her from the spot where he still sat on the landing. Her face was tight and closed, the muscles around her jaw visible, every line wound tight. He got up and walked towards her. She leaned, still clutching his coat, against the wall beside the door. He had been wrong or else her eyes had lightened with her worry. Jake could make out pupils now, two black circles which shook and danced.

"Why did you come here?" she asked.

The hand he held out for his jacket floated awkwardly in the space between them. "I'm trying to find some things out about my father. His past."

"Well, as you could see, your guess is as good as hers."

"I see that now, I'm sorry for intruding."

Her hand gripped and turned the doorknob but she didn't open it. Instead, she stopped and held the door in limbo.

"I know you think you can judge her for what she did, but she didn't have a choice." Unfolding her arms, she held out his jacket and watched as he slipped it over his shoulders. Cold air swarmed the foyer through the open sliver and Jake hastened to button his coat.

"Sorry?" The oversized buttons resisted his push through thick wool buttonholes.

"She has no reason to feel bad or guilty. If she hadn't done what she did, hid who she was, none of us would be here. You can't make her feel bad for that."

"I didn't mean to make her feel bad. If I did, I'm sorry."

She stared at Jake, watched him fumble with his collar, unsure of whether or not to believe him, afraid of what cracks the afternoon had opened in her grandmother. "She used to tell us made-up stories when we were kids. Animal stories, about a tiger named Bonzo she wanted to keep as a pet, keep safe, but couldn't. About how she could wash the tiger as much as she wanted, soap and scrubbing, and cover him in coats of paint in all different colours. But his stripes would always show through. She said they came from the inside and so the smart hunter, the one with keen eyes, no matter what, would always be able to find him anyway. It's no fun to be a tiger. No fun to love one either."

———————

Flakes of bedroom paint bloomed out from the metal box propped in his open window. Rose said the room was chosen just for him because it had the best window in the entire house: southern exposure and on the second floor so he could see into the backyard, over the fences into the yards of both of his neighbours, and right across the small park behind the house. The perfect view. It was the only window in his room, as wide as young Jake's full arm span and up less than a meter above the floor. Standing in socked feet, he used to be able to look out and take in every inch of his suburban vista. But that was before Ike put in the air conditioning unit, the squat angry wood-panelled unit that was in there now. The wooden sill was not very long, and so Ike, never the handyman, had screwed metal brackets into the wall underneath the window to help support the thing. Jake was nonplussed about the improvement. It sat there, leaning back, relaxed, obstructing his view.

Young Jake pulled his desk chair as close to the window as he could get, its legs stumbling across the nubbly carpet. Sitting on crossed knees, Jake leaned as far as he could on the perched unit and stared outside. He was sure he could hear the voices of his friends playing in the park or in the street. In fact, he distinctly made out the happy chatter of every single kid in his class, maybe even his entire grade, playing and enjoying their summer vacation in the fresh air. There was a game of baseball in the park. He wiped the back of his hand against his cheek and settled back into his chair. It was better the other kids didn't see him, up here in his room. The one thing worse than being inside studying during the best part of the summer would be their pity.

Ignoring the open French book and the blank lined pages of his scribbler, Jake snuck into the hallway and made his way downstairs. Rose was in the kitchen fixing the hem in a dark purple skirt. She sat at the table, carefully folding an edge into the cloth, her threaded needle primed and held between clenched teeth. Jake let his little body drop heavily into the chair beside her. Rose bent her head slightly towards her son and gave him a wink before returning her eyes to her task.

"Is he home yet?"

Rose dropped the needle from her lips into her open hand and lined its head up with her seam. "If yes, would you be out of your room?"

"Maybe." He slumped into the table, his shoulders pressed against the tabletop's edge and his arms dangling beneath, on either side of his chair. "It's not fair. I learn French in school like everyone else and Hebrew for hours and hours afterwards. Everyone gets a summer break but me."

Jake knew that even if his mother wanted to, she could not excuse him from his summer studies. It had been his father's decision, his father's decree, and only Ike could let him out of it.

"Oh my, you sound like a prisoner. It's only a few hours a week, *boychik*." She nudged him with her elbow. Jake placed a finger at the crux of her last stitch, and she tied the knot over and around his hand. "*Zey opleygn lamdones nor vos, badoyeven batsoln shpeter.*" Those who put off learning now, pay sorely for it later.

The more Jake repeated the question, the more frustrated he became with his father's answer. Stars had already replaced clouds in the sky when Ike and Jake sat together in the boy's bedroom. Jake's legs and arms stretched out across the rumpled sheets of his bed while Ike sat in the desk chair pulled close beside his son, the fabric of his pant legs bunching against the mattress.

"But why? I have to study all year."

"A little extra never hurt anyone. I heard your French and your friends'. It's not enough. You could barely get by."

"I don't need to get by. I speak English like everyone else."

"Not everyone, Jacob."

"I do it good enough and besides," Jake reached under his bed and pulled out the fat reference book with its yellow and red cover, the corners of the grainy pages bent at different angles in different directions, "I can just use a dictionary. Or ask a French person for help."

"Not good enough."

Jake threw the dictionary down on the floor near his father's feet. With the rounded tip of his loafers, Ike slid the book back into hiding under the bed. "You need to know every word, hear them, and know them for yourself. You should not have to trust other people to make it clear to you. To fill in the spaces."

Ike did his best to explain. There are other spaces in between words than those white and visible on the page, than the vacant breath between syllables. There is wide unmarked terrain, open space between the mouth and the ear, and the ear and the brain, where meaning is decided. Ike told his son that he remembered how different the same news would look coming from his father or his mother — only by knowing the words could he tell whose face to believe.

Without speaking it, his mind's eye was clouded by a memory: the first time he heard the word for Jew in French; the store clerk's face twisted, spittle landing on the counter between them. He would not have known and had no idea if Zalman not been there to interpret for him, pointing to the sign by the door. The words on the sign and the face of the clerk, and the voice in his head, repeating one word over and over again. *Loyfn*. Run.

"The universe of difference sits in the between. Some people in Poland speak both Yiddish and Polish, but for everyone else, even though they come from the same place, it is very hard to understand each other."

He tried to track some revelation in the style of his son's face, the contour of his shoulders. He offered his son an example. It was like Rose and her sayings.

"In Yiddish: *kluge kinder hobn kurtse jorn* means that wise children have short years. The words in Polish — *madre dzieci nie uchowaja sie* — say that wise children have short lives. In Yiddish, it speaks that wise children are not long allowed to be children. But in Polish, it promises for an early death."

"So," his son asked, "which one is it? Which one is true?"

A crackle of paint came off with her fingernail where she picked at the wall beneath the window.

Jake and Seda were following her in and out of each room in his father's house. It felt invasive, Jake watching as this real estate agent poked and prodded his apparently decrepit childhood home. The first thing she said to them upon meeting in the driveway was that the whole exterior would need a facelift. He had almost laughed out loud. Seda, reading his mind, stepped in and directed the woman to the front door. "We were hoping to focus more on the inside." The agent walked in ahead of them as Seda leaned over and whispered into his ear, "If your father weren't already dead, this may have killed him."

They had reached Jake's bedroom. The walls were the same boyish blue they had always been, only the colour was faded, and a bad roof leak had left bubbles in three of the four walls. "It needs a fresh coat, something neutral. This view is wonderful though." She drew on the blinds until they scaled the full height of the window. "Nice view of the yard. The short fence is a bit of an issue. Whoever takes it will have to build up." She turned and smiled at Seda, the smile of a cohort, woman to woman, "I mean no one wants to be able to see in everyone's backyard, especially if it means they can see into yours."

The three of them made their way again, back downstairs. Still full of furniture and yet emptied of all of its most personal possessions, Jake, too, began to see the house like an old woman. The age spots, walls which had over the years been thoughtlessly over-exposed to the sun streaming in from windows. Spider veins of well-worn paths that criss-crossed her carpets and floors. The master bedroom still had his father's bed in it and the one unadorned nightstand. The dining room table and living room set were where they always were. But his mother's art was off the walls, his father's books cleared from shelves, and every family photo, every frame, sat wrapped in bubble wrap in the storage locker at Jake's apartment.

Even the basement was nothing but a sad desk, table, and chair. "Now this is a plus." The real estate agent ran her hand along the unpainted drywall. "A semi-finished basement, a blank slate. It makes it more of a family home. Lots of possibilities." For the first time since coming inside, she addressed Jake directly. "We could stage it as a family playroom."

Later that week, Jake lingered over every detail as he described the whole ridiculous scene over lunch. "Vapid, Leah. The word is vapid." He watched her push away her plate before lighting a cigarette. She held it clumsily between the index and middle finger of her right hand, doing her best not to drop it while attempting to strike a match with the remaining fingers.

"Judgemental, Jake. The word is judgemental." Finally successful, she puffed her now-lit cigarette several times before taking it out of her mouth and waving her hand at the waitress for the bill. "Besides, she's a real estate agent. What do you expect from someone whose profession deems the best advertising possible to be their face plastered on a bus bench? Seriously, your face under a stranger's ass while they wait for a bus as a means to sell houses."

"A good point. So, what is this?" He pointed at the smoke escaping from the underside of the table where her cigarette and hand were resting.

"It's newish. Part of a new lifestyle."

"You on a health kick there, Leah?"

"Of sorts. It's an appetite suppressant."

He laughed. "That's just sad." With her left hand, she pushed the rising smoke away from her face. "And what are you doing?"

"I hate the way it smells." She tugged on her ponytail. "And it gets in my hair."

He pushed the ashtray closer to her across the small circular table, "I take it back. That is beyond sad."

Leah squinted her eyes, faking annoyance in response. Their lunch date, to catch up on what he was missing at work, had gone as well as most previous business meetings. That is to say that very little business had been done. "I think Seda's right and you're ridiculous to be in a hurry to sell the place anyway." Another single puff and the cigarette disappeared again. "You should take some time, let the dust settle."

"Months, Leah. Months plural. The dust is settled. At this point, it's just another something I have to take care of."

She shrugged and flipped through the dessert menu that sat between them. It had been months since Ike's death, almost three. The dirt over his body, swathed in white, would have been long hardened, the seams of his burial stitched close and erased under the frost. Perhaps it was morbid but every time Seda suggested they visit the cemetery, it was all that would come to Jake's mind — at first, when they put Ike in the ground, which was colder: his own body frozen and dead or the chilled December earth, so heavy and clumsy on Jake's shovel? Of course, he didn't speak it; it was not the type of thing you say. Rather he would tell her that there was nothing there yet for them to do, no headstone to lay a rock on, nothing above ground which could let him know that his father was really under there at all. It was a good answer, even if it was a lie. He'd planned for the unveiling early, or as early as Jewish custom and the cemetery allowed. His father's headstone had already been stood up. It was there now, unadorned. Unacknowledged.

Jake watched his friend while the waitress cleared away their plates, the wax paper which sat under the remains of their Wilenski's Specials see-through and slick with grease on the plate. "How much do you know about your family's history?"

"Other than that I'm a complete Eastern European mutt and all the extended relatives on both sides of the family look alarmingly similar?" Shrugging again, she pressed the butt hard into the ashtray, dabbing several times to squash every ember. "I don't know. Not much. Enough. They all tell stories all the time. You know, it's what they do. What's a family if there's no legacy to go along with it?" Leah reached down and lifted her foot up onto the seat beneath her, perching on the one crossed leg. "When I was a kid, I asked my grandfather where in Russia he came from, and he told me that it was called *hivneh*. I had to look it up in a dictionary; it turns out the word means 'shit hole.' Other than that, I read a lot of Isaac Bashevis Singer. I dated a Phish-head."

Jake chuckled, his cheeks pinking with the effort. It was

why he had always been so drawn to her as his only Jewish friend since high school. Something about finally being on the inside of the inside joke.

"I don't know, Jake. They waited a long time to talk about it. My grandmother wouldn't even say the word 'Nazi' until she felt pretty sure every last one of them she knew personally was dead." Distracted, she traced the picture of black forest cake on the dessert menu with her index finger, over and over, her fingertip smudging the plastic cover. Looking up at him, she shrugged, changing the subject of her own thoughts. "I've been meaning to ask, before I forget..." Hesitant, she pulled her purse off the corner of her seat back and began to fiddle with its zipper in her lap. "I was wondering what you were doing for the holidays?" Her face still bent downward, Leah looked up at him from under her eyelashes. "Passover is coming up and I figured you hadn't thought much about it, but I wanted to invite you, for the first night or the second. You and Seda, of course. You know my mother would love to have you again, it's been a couple of years. We can make Seda ask the Four Questions."

"Thanks." Jake allowed himself to smile for her. Reaching into his pocket and pulling out his wallet, he laid enough money on the table to cover the whole of the bill. "I'll let you know."

———————

The envelope had stood out among the ripped edges and folded newsprint that filled Ike's folder. It was complete: the lip slit carefully open by the clean edge of a letter opener and the ivory coloured paper still plump with the letter inside. Even the notched edges of the stamp, almost exactly thirty-five years later, stuck smooth and pressed in the top right corner. Looking closely, Jake could make out thin strips of pencil — ruler-made lines upon which the meticulous letters of both the intended and return address sat. Even the paper hidden inside was neatly creased and tucked.

The envelope was addressed to "Mr. and Mrs. I. Langley c/o The Canadian Jewish Chronicle," but the only page it contained, written in the same tidy hand, began with the words: "*Lib Yitzhak.*" Dear Isaac...

> *I worried a bit to start this way. But it is both my affection and my hello.*
>
> *It was equally thrill and relief to see your name in the paper. I knew it was you right away, missing letters and all. I wonder how quickly you will recognize me. I cannot bear to think you wouldn't remember. And how happy I was to learn of your simcha. News of your happiness increases my own. Mazel tov, mazel tov Yitzhak mayn. And to Rose, as well.*

The writing goes on, briefly describing her life, a husband, children. *So much of my own it breaks my heart sometimes to think about it.* The page ends with another warm congratulations and a signature: simply *Mina*. It seemed silly to Jake that she would ask if Ike knew her; her full name and address were printed so clearly on the outside of the envelope. Only for a minute did it occur to him that for this woman writing to this man there was more than a name to remember. Reading it was like stepping into the middle of a private conversation, slipping between spoken words where naturally a breath would be taken. *I want to tell you what has been but even in letters I want to speak softly. Our stories, like yours and mine, are whispering ones.* He read the letter over and over but did not share it with Seda or anyone else.

———————

"I hear his voice now."

"You are now hearing voices."

"In my head, Zalman. More and more, I hear his voice. Things he said or didn't, but would.

"Growing up, it was always only my mother. Like my brain was filling in the gaps where she should have been. Because she should've been there. Little things, every day, her voice would just be there, out of nowhere. And now him."

Jake let the silence sit between them on the phone. It felt natural, as these calls were becoming more and more frequent, more and more natural. He waited for Zalman to ask a follow up, prying for more details the way other people would. Instead, the old man waited, no doubt equally lost in thought. Finally, a question asked, a change of subject.

"So, have you decided? If so, you should buy your tickets soon."

קלוגע קינדער

WISE CHILDREN

§

Teves 5699

January 1939

It is the third day of a new year for everyone else; for us the same year continues moving slowly along. Mina has a cousin who speaks Polish. He told her that January means rod: a pole shoved into the frozen earth that proclaims, "Everything will start here. The whole rest of the year will pivot around this point. This rod is where 1939 began." This is not Mina's favourite—this month nor its meaning. She prefers November, the month of falling leaves, and June, which means worms. Mina lists for me the words she knows: the months in Polish, words to describe weather (*potraw* for fog, *burzowy* for stormy, *grzmot* for thunder) and words about luck and omens, too (*stracony* is doomed). She can even speak a little in Russian: коровa is the cow which walks in the farmer's полевой, field. Her brother Aaron covers his ears and rolls his eyes back into his head while she speaks, mouthing the words *kluger nudnik* to me across the table. Aaron teases his big sister, but Mina doesn't seem to mind. She just shakes her head and smiles at him, and then she turns and smiles at me. Aaron is too young to appreciate our conversations though she is endlessly patient with him; the whole Rosenberg family is patient with their youngest son, but Mina is the kindest.

I don't mind listening to Mina speak about other languages; I have no relatives from Warsaw who can teach me such things. I try to memorize the words as she speaks them. I concentrate on her mouth's determined forming of each sound and spin the tone of her voice speaking over and over in my head.

Uncle loves this place. He feels as welcome at the Rosenbergs' as I do, but that is not why he is so happy here.

The large shul is in the west end of the city; it is where we must do our work. The Rosenbergs live in the neighbourhood that sits on the eastern tip of the city. Aaron and the other boys attend school close to their home, so Uncle and I make our journey just the two of us. The long walk to the shul in the cold deepens our breath; each one is a thick burst of hot air that lays a layer of moist droplets on the tip of our mufflers. The feel of the wet wool rubbing just beneath my lower lip makes me shudder more than the cold. Uncle and I walk and breathe at the same pace, pushing towards the shul. When its massive stone walls come into clear view, when the lower buildings have passed and we step amid the stalls of the marketplace, Uncle changes pace and stride. He holds his breath in for just a moment longer, his stride shortens, and he allows both of his hands to swing by his sides and his muffler slip down below his chin.

We have walked this path for four days now and

each day it is the same. I hold my own breath; let the air out smoother and softer, lowering its volume inside my own ears, anticipating his change. I have heard it in him before, this shift, the way his breathing changes when he is telling stories. When he is remembering, as if he must savour every part of it, even the air in his own lungs. I understand it: the outside of this shul looks very much like our shul back home. The same three-tiered wooden roof with each tier sloping down and out before rising in a tip to the sky. The lowest tier grazes the walls of the shul, like the path of a swooping bird mapped out in wood, narrowly making its escape over the high walls.

Uncle points to the clutter of the marketplace cozied up against the thick stonewalls, "The Temple was like this, all things together as they should be. What you see is a ladder planted in our everyday soul that stretches towards the heavens. Everyone here shuffles back and forth between the angels and the marketplace." Today, he is in an especially good mood because it is *Shabbas*.

There is a slope of smaller stones and rubble that lines the back wall of the shul. The *genizah* is buried in behind these stones in the building's foundation. It is only accessible through an outside passageway that is hidden by the rocks, big enough only for a small boy to enter. Each morning we must dig through the stones to reveal its thin oval opening. (It is hidden and yet every-day people from the market watch us expose it. I thought we should be more secretive at first, but Uncle said,

"This is the Jewish market, only our kind are behind these walls. And it should be no secret from them.") I am too tall and so the rabbi's son must help us, carrying the books and papers out almost one at a time as the space is barely big enough for him to move through unburdened. He is only six and doesn't speak very much. His father brings him to us each morning as we wait behind the shul. Uncle and I collect what the boy fetches, and we move the papers inside the building to do our sorting.

Although it is colder than ever, a heavy frost having followed us into this place, my favourite time is spent outside waiting for the boy to come out of the *genizah*. My back presses hard against the frozen stone. I lean against the shul's wall where two of the giant slabs of stone meet; I can just barely make out the roughness of the grout beneath my many layers of clothing. The rabbi's voice is a fuzzy backdrop to this perfect morning; he speaks to my uncle and a small group of men soon gathers around them. Laughter breaks out from the middle of the circle, and I can make out that one of the men has a terrible lisp. Shifting my weight, I slide across the smooth wall away from the group. Their voices soon join the jumble of sounds coming from the market. Hairs prick up on the back of my neck as I let my skin rest against the cool stones; the sensation is refreshing while the rest of me sweats beneath these heavy clothes. Friday is my favourite day, too.

She stands at the edge of the table beside her mother and waits for the wicks to catch light. Covering her eyes, her lips move at one with the other women: *baruch ata adonai ...* The words of the prayer melt away. Mina's lips quicken in their movement, her eyes still shrouded by her hands, she speaks a silent prayer for her family. All the women do the same as we men watch and wait. When she finishes, Mina looks down at the candles. Her shawl tonight is a deep red, woven wide so that the colours of her blouse just barely sneak through. The other women finish and sit. Mr. Rosenberg uncovers the challah and invites my uncle, as his guest, to bless it. When he is done, Uncle tears a large chunk off the braided bread and passes it around the table.

With food on every plate, Aaron offers to sing a song. The family laughs and Mr. Rosenberg turns to my uncle and me, "Every *Shabbas*, he sings for us something new. He picks them up at school." Uncle laughs, his mouth spread wide and open across his face, "So nothing has changed in school then from when I was his age." His shoulders bounce softly up and down as his laughter joins the general raucous at the table. My own cheeks begin to ache from smiling. One of the other Rosenberg children pipes up, "Perhaps this time he'll remember the whole song and not have to repeat lines because he forgot the words." Mrs. Rosenberg urges Aaron to stand up, lightly pulling on his sleeve, "Don't listen to them, you do a wonderful job." Dipping a piece of challah into my broth, I lean back in my chair. I let myself laugh out loudwhen Uncle puts his arm around me. The little boy stands beside his chair and prepares to sing, drawing in a breath so deep it looks for a moment like he might fall over.

———

Emptied by the day, my body is motionless with sleep and yet my mind cannot stop. I listen to the deep rumble coming from my uncle beside me, his sound tapping every wall and surface, the room alive with his breathing. In my bed, with the dark ceiling hovering above me and both my eyes open, I picture her mouth and move my lips to form the unfamiliar words with her. "*Mrok*... darkness."

———

"He'll have to go. Mina, you are being ridiculous. It is no worse than it has ever been. And it is not your place to speak on the matter at all. I have allowed you too many liberties already. Aaron goes to school today like every other day." Paths of glossy wet skin trip down Mina's cheeks, a sliver of her body visible through the crack in the door. She stands in the middle of the kitchen while Aaron and I crouch together behind the front door, unnoticed. Mr. Rosenberg stands in front of her, his hands held in fists, pressed against the sides of her face.

Aaron's face has collapsed beside me, his lashes wet

from crying, "I can show her its okay. I'm brave, she doesn't have to get in trouble for me." His back is turned against the door so that he cannot see his sister but has heard his father's gentle tone. Mina whispers now, and the sound is muffled; her head rests on her father's shoulder, her face turned towards him so that all I can see is the braid of light brown hair that swings at her side.

"I know," Mr. Rosenberg has one fist pressed against his daughter's back and the other resting on his own forehead. "But it would do us no good to hide. It would do no good for him."

It takes a moment for me to understand that he is not hurting her, grasping her like that, but rather holding her up.

———

"I'll do my chores outside while I wait for Aaron to wake up. You can keep me company." Mina's eyes are red from her crying but otherwise her face shows no mark of what has gone on today. Today, Sunday, the sky has been unusually clear, and I am happy to follow her out behind the house. I was the only one surprised by what happened...what I saw. It caused a headache to plant itself behind my eyes and I'm hoping the fresh air will break up the pain. Mina saw it too but did not cry right away; she waited until after he was asleep and could not hear her.

Just before Aaron had come home, I'd accidentally

interrupted her in the kitchen. I had been looking for her, hoping for one of our conversations, eager to show her how many of her strange words I had learned. She stopped washing dishes when she heard me come into the kitchen. She stopped but didn't turn around. I watched her and wondered how a woman's back, just her back, could look so sad. Using her wet hands to brush the bubbles of soap down into the basin, moving them along and over the inside of her wrists, she said only "He walks to school carrying rocks in his fists...all my brothers do. But the stones get heavy and Aaron always lets them go too early. He never makes it all the way there."

———

Hours later, the afternoon sunlight lends the air an appearance of warmth but in truth it is razor-like in its cold. Mina moves as if oblivious to its sting, pulling sopping clothing from a bucket of steaming water. "Most days the older boys walk with him. On Sundays, he leaves early and walks home with a friend, the others staying on for more study. The two of them are supposed to walk through the main streets and stay where it's crowded. He gets so distracted though; he wanders. And on Sundays it is the worst."

She brushes a wayward drift of snow from her sleeve and her words hang before her in soft white clouds. She stands between her bucket of clean washing and a large woven basket of dry clothes she has brought out to air. Watching her, I feel as if I know what she means, though what happened today is still so unreal. I have seen so much of her today: tears, at first concerned turn angry, poise regained while a bloodied younger brother lies sleeping. And sadness, hiding itself on her face, yet blooms everywhere else on her body.

Her speaking brings me back to her, "Usually it's other boys, little ones, like him or a little older. But children, at least. Not today. Never on days like today." Mina moves quickly, facing away from me, ringing the clothing out, using her fingers to pull the water from the fabric in long strong strokes. I am presented with a glimpse of the side of her face, only for a moment. I cannot read what is on it. The knuckles of her hands and the tips of her fingers are red and cracked; they look raw against the rest of her hands, which have lost any colour at all. With every movement, I wince: they look so brittle and frozen that with each bend I fear they will snap. "What happens today, Mina?" Her thin red and white fingers halt in their task before falling down at her sides. Twisting her bulky skirt and long jacket to the side, Mina lets her body slump down on top of the pile of dry clothes in her basket.

"They go to church, hear what their leaders have to say and then go outside the town to get drunk. But they always come back. Not boys. Young men. You can smell them coming. Onions, vodka, and garlic. I smelled them once and now I can smell them in my sleep. They're worked up, furious because their holy men reminded them to hate the Jewish murderers." She turns her head towards me, only enough so that she can rest her chin on her shoulder. I can see the grey-green in her eyes though we are more than a foot apart. "Imagine that." Her eyes slip into mine, "Beating up a little boy for a death in their book."

———

When Aaron sleeps, he reminds me of Ben. Their blankets and sheets are a tangled mess, and they lie there, curled up with their knees against their chests, like bumps at the centre of the twisted fabric.

———

The walls of the buildings, the men and women in the street, foreign words circling around us — everything looks different this morning. There is a change today, something new. Uncle and I do not slow our pace until we reach the shul's doors. I do not look up as I walk, watching the movement and direction of Uncle's feet beside me, making my own feet move the same way. His quickened steps leave deep caverns in the fluffy snow that fell all through last night. At breakfast, Mr. Rosenberg said that a fresh sweeping of snow was a good sign, signalling a fresh start for the coming week. His wife and Uncle had nodded, but none of the children seemed to be listening. None of them seemed to have heard. I heard but I didn't nod because I didn't agree. I don't see what difference falling snow could make; after all, falling is what snow does and its landing in the middle of winter seems like no big sign or miracle to me. Uncle does not breathe deep today and does not savour any moment of our journey. The clatter of the market is harsh, bearing down on us until the heavy doors of the shul close behind us, mercifully shutting everything out.

Our papers wait for us at a table to the right of the arc. Behind the wooden platform is a mural: scripture painted onto the wall, black letters in a copper frame. It is hard to make out the pattern painted inside the thick frame; the plaster of the old wall has absorbed the paint, making the lines of the figures blur. The wall is crumbling in other places, black letters missing or broken where the wall is chipped. At the top of the frame is a small arch and above that sits a dark golden crown arched over the name of the Lord, bold and black Over the ark is a plaster archway, also adorned with scripture. Its columns are an ocean of faded blue, striped with copper paint. The legs of the chairs set up at our table, pulled from beside the ark, are painted to match. Our table sits beneath one of the room's three candelabra chandeliers; the rest of the light comes from the large windows near the ceiling, sunlight sent in splinters throughout the room, cut by the steel bars in front of the glass.

Uncle rests his hands on top of the pile of papers and eases himself into his chair. He signals me to pull my chair by him, dropping his head to the side and turning over his right hand so its palm faces the empty space beside him. The scraping of the chair's stubby wooden legs across the stone floor breaks the room's silence. I sit and neither of us speaks; Uncle opens a rectangular book with a faded silver cover that sits on top of the others. It is thin and must not have been stored well: the edges of the paper are crinkled, and brown smudges spread out across the pages as signs of water damage...dirty water. Forever seems to pass while he gazes lazily at every page.

Near to him, my eyes follow his across the papers, but I take nothing in. Instead, I let the noise from outside return to me; I seek it out in the silence as drops of it come in through the high windows. "I have been meaning to speak with you. I know we needn't discuss yesterday, you understand everything already, don't you?" He speaks but does not turn to me. The way his eyes refuse to stop on any word, any character on the page, tells me that he, too, is not paying attention to what he reads. Turning one page over for the next, he waits for me to answer.

"I do, I think I do. Mina spoke to me about it, what goes on here," I slip my hands beneath me, hoping that my weight pressing them against the seat will keep them from shaking, "I understand."

"Then you understand more than me. To me, it does not make sense at all."

"I didn't mean... It is just with everything..."

"Yitzhak, do you know what it is to make one's home in the den of the beast?" I pause, for a moment considering but Uncle does not wait, "You settle, build houses. Get used to the sound of the monster's breathing, his heat beside you, his shadow over everything. And you pretend that because you can tolerate his taking up so much room, that he will be willing to tolerate your presence there, too. But it's not always so, and one day, he decides he does not like your being there at all." I say nothing, waiting for him to continue. I don't understand, I don't know what he means. "This is a dangerous place for our people to be, so close, pushed up against their world. It is wiser to make our homes away from them."

Uncle places his hand on my shoulder and with it, turns me and pulls me towards him. Our faces are now bent closely together as if we are whispering in secret. "To live separately. To not tempt the monster at all."

————

In this place, there have been three New Years. Three beginnings. Rosh Hashanah, when we began to count our months from the start again – *Tishri, Cheshvan, Kislev, Tevet...* Our lunar months and days and years, 5699 of them. Their New Year, their marking of time, 1939. And that day: our fifteenth of *Cheshvan*, their early November. Not so long ago...not so long ago now. It marked the beginning of something too. I can feel it.

———

Sunset approaches and the streets are filled with the tides of men making their way home for dinner. Uncle and I move within the pack. The narrow streets near the shul, only wide enough for people on foot or small push-wagons, spill into the broad streets that curve through the heart of the city. We must cross this entire place to reach the Rosenbergs. The crowd makes it easy to move quickly, past rectangular buildings with thick glass windows, stores with Polish names, even a few cars looking out of place against these walls, swarmed by this mob. Everyone seems to be heading in the same direction.

Uncle and I walk close together, our arms brushing now and again, the sounds of wool grazing wool. It is an easy place to get lost. At the heart of the city, the men begin to spread out, dropping off, each heading down the particular path that will take him home. Just past the Polish school, in the eastern corner of the city, is the neighbourhood where the Rosenbergs live. There is an invisible line here, beyond which the shapes of the houses change and a few *mezuzot* can still be seen nailed onto doorframes.

It was here that Aaron decided to walk the rest of the way without his friend. They had left *cheder* late, distracted by a game being played by some of the other children on the front steps. Aaron's friend was nervous that they had lingered too long and would both be in trouble for being late and making their mothers worry. The boys decided they should split up, each taking the shortest route home. Aaron's friend was nervous about going alone, so Aaron waited, watching him go down the street before turning left, heading down the road that skims the edge of the city. It was his shortcut home, and now it is the road along which Uncle and I make our way.

No longer carried by a crowd's momentum, there is time to really notice what is around me. Not more than twenty steps, and we seem to have left the large city completely. With houses to our left, the area on the right side of the road opens up into white frosted field that is crisscrossed here and there by wooden fences. Near one fence, a deep trough cuts the thick pile of snow, the path of someone crossing the field on foot.

This is where they surrounded him. He remembers there being three of them, said there were at least three because that was the number of faces he saw—the number of voices he remembers. They must have yelled at him to stop, encouraged each other, and then cheered or grunted when they hit him. Aaron didn't understand anything they said but he understood what they wanted.

The first face — the one with curly hair — spat on him before pushing him to the ground. (This must be where he landed in the snow. Yes, there is a dent here in the shape of a boy.)

151

The second face — he remembers black eyes — kicked him so hard in the stomach that doubling forward, his *kippah* fell off. (Imagine that, remembering something like that.

But it was the third face — the one he cannot recall — that made him start bleeding. (There is no blood here. He mostly bled on himself. That was the face he said never stopped yelling, yelling in his ear, shaking him and hitting him at the same time, shouting so loud. That was the face that was last to leave, the other two marching off while he waited for Aaron to move, to see if he moved. That last face waited and stayed to watch as Aaron got up and tried to run away.

Looking ahead, I can just make out a band of the Rosenbergs' chimney. Standing right here, right where I am (where he was)I can see it. We will be there soon.

At our speed, with our grown-up legs, we will reach there very soon.

————

For the past several days she has moved around this place like a paper woman: fragile, see-through, barely there. But Aaron got up yesterday, being his first day out of bed since it happened. And she came back a little. Today was his first day back at school; she wrung her hands behind his back in the kitchen, watching him put his jacket on and tie his shoes. We stood together at the window, staring out until he moved beyond our view.

I could almost feel her fill-out beside me. Her mood was up and down while he was gone, every hour swinging between relief and worry. Then, not too long ago, we heard his voice cry out, "Mina, Mama, we're home." And for the first time since it happened, Mina smiled and was entirely here again.

"If you're leaving when your uncle says you plan to, you must be nearly done at the shul."

"All we have left to do is prepare the *shemot* for burial." I hand her another log of wood for the fire. "And that is almost ready."

Mina brushes slivers of bark off her skirt onto the floor beside the stove. With her foot she sweeps them into a pile with the others, the tip of her black leather boot nudging the wood gently into a mound. "I wish I could come. I would like to watch."

"It's simple and short. Not much ceremony." I pull out a chair for her at the kitchen table. Without turning, she backs up and eases herself into it, keeping her eyes on the fire to make sure the new log fully catches. A long hissing moves toward us from inside the fire, followed by a low pop and loud crackle as the fresh log lights up with flames. I realize I have been standing behind her all this time, my hands still lingering on the back of her chair. I move around the table to sit across from her.

Gripping the tabletop, I tuck myself tightly in

towards the table so close now that it presses uncomfortably into my ribs, crossing my arms on its cool surface. Mina turns to face me and does the same, her body a mirror of mine against the wood; "Of course there is ceremony. You are placing *shemot* in holy ground. The rabbi will be there to see the letters be covered with dirt. Once there, they will last forever." Rumbling, cracking sounds continue to pour from the fire. "If I asked you, you would tell me where they had been buried, right?" A strand of coffee-coloured hair has slipped out of her *babushkah*; it curls twice, in large loops, before touching down on her shoulder. She is wearing blue again. My favourite colour. I nod to her my reply: *of course.* "Then I think I shall visit them, after you are gone. I will place stones."

"Why, Mina?" I cannot help but say her name.
"Even words on paper deserve to be remembered."
Perhaps she feels the hair brushing against the thin skin of her ear lobe for she collects it, winding it around her finger and tucking it back beneath cloth, "That way there is something everlasting above ground as well as beneath."

———

Our bags packed and at our side, there is no need to return to the Rosenbergs from the cemetery before we leave. Besides, others are travelling with us, and it would not be right to keep them waiting. The rabbi and Mr.

Rosenberg walk us to the road where the wagon sits. Four boys, most of them younger than me, are already piled on. The rabbi says they are going to attend the *yeshivah* in Kutno. They will travel with us and follow us through our next few stops on our way there. The rabbi promises they will stay out of our way, but it is not a good time for them to be travelling alone. He tells us that more than one boy has been attacked on the roads outside the city. Uncle lets out a low grunt and slowly shakes his head. "There is no reason they cannot make their way with us. I hope to be in Kutno soon enough anyhow." Their slow goodbye, hugs from Mr. Rosenberg, his best wishes from each member of his family, grate on me. My ears burn hot red as I load our bags onto the wagon. This is the worst time for extra company. I want to get going, but Uncle insists on saying what seems like a hundred farewells.

Finally, we're moving. The four boys sit in a circle behind us, their voices are nervous, barely louder than a whisper. I pretend I am trying to listen; Uncle watches me tip my head towards them. I push my eyes down into a squint and flatten the line of my mouth. Sighing, Uncle pats my knee with mock disapproval and turns his attention to the scenery that rocks past us on either side. In truth, nothing about the boys interests me. Despite the chilly evening air, the skin on my back is slick with sweat and the wobbling of the wagon, side to side, is echoed in the tossing of my stomach. A swell of lightheadedness overtakes me, and I rest my head against the prickly fabric of Uncle's jacket sleeve. He must think I have given up trying to listen over the noise of our ride and decided to try sleep instead. He rests his head against mine. I feel sleep come over him, the way his weight shifts towards me. Tilting my head slightly, peering up I can see the motion of his Adam's apple move with the up and down of old man swallowing timed to the quivering suspension of old man snores.

I slide my hand between the buttons of my jacket and move it along my chest until it finds the fold of my vest. The whole time we were at the cemetery and on the walk to the wagon, I was sure I would lose it — that it would slip out and I might not notice, or worse that someone else would. When Mr. Rosenberg hugged me goodbye so tight I was convinced that somehow he would feel it between us and know what had been done. I haven't lost it, though; it is safe. Tucked inside the hole in my vest's lining, the hole I slit with a knife Mina took from her kitchen. The paper is so small and thin, I can only be sure it is safe when my fingers find and trace its edges. Afraid the weight of my finger's touch might make the note dissolve, disappear, as if it had never been, I pull my hand away and try to sleep.

When she first gave it to me, the paper still smelled of her hands: rose water soap. She said it was a gift from her to only me, the letters so perfect and smooth, the *mem* tilted every so slightly to the right. A square torn neatly from my journal, it reads simply "Mina."

§

Mina was easy enough to find. The address on the envelope was no longer hers, but her current phone number was listed. This time, this stranger, had known him immediately and had stopped Jake before he tried to explain: "Yes, Jacob, Isaac's son. Your father told me often about you." That weekend would be no good for a visit, but soon, if he could come to Toronto, she would love to meet him. "And it will give me time," she said, her voice excited and quick, her accent glazing over the lilt of her words. "I think I have something to show you." He would drive in during the week. It was good; she rarely had visitors then.

He chose to take the Bathurst exit off of the highway. The street was speckled here and there with quickie nail salons and kosher bakeries. Jake slowed to stare in shop windows and read billboards. To his right, cursive maroon letters arched over a wide storefront window framing a mannequin with arms and legs tastefully covered, a sign that read "Frumela's." It was one of the landmarks Mina had mentioned, and only one detail of random information set out on a yellow post-it he had pressed to the Toronto street map and suggested route he had printed out and stuffed in his glove box. Turning right down Mina's avenue, Jake began counting street corners. The map told him that it was only a few blocks in, and Mina had warned that if he went too far it would be tricky to turn around and come back her way.

With an institutional brick exterior and brown metal window frames, the long-term care facility blended seamlessly into the 1970s façade of small shops and restaurants on the block. The stucco lobby jutted out from its side like a ridiculous afterthought, creating the Eastern corner of a shovelled brick courtyard. Mina said she would give his name to the people at the front desk and tell them he was expected. Veering left after moving through the front doors, Jake took the steps into the main lobby, avoiding the soft-sloping ramp that hugged the walls and poured out into the room's centre. Pinevale Terrace's name seemed inspired by the lobby décor; the evergreen carpet went with the overstuffed armchairs and complementary dark floral curtains, and the pine-stained furniture matched perfectly the pine-stained banisters and railings.

Only the beige melamine front desk was out of place, the heavyset woman behind it informing Jake that indeed Mrs. Birnbaum was expecting him. "You'll just need to put your name in here. Are you just dropping by or planning on staying a little while?"

Jake signed the visitor's log. "A few hours maybe."

"That should be fine. She's having a good day, but she's in and out when she gets tired. She's a little fragile. You can go straight up to her room."

A latticework of framed pictures spread out across each of the suite's four walls. In the corner beside her bed, a cluster of loose snapshots — children, teenagers, and babies — was tacked to the wall. There were a couple of chairs placed in front of the small television and Jake had sat in the smaller of the two. Even with her dyed brown hair teased above her head, Mina looked shrunken inside the arms of the wing chair in which she sat. She had a smoker's face with the dramatic bow of her cheeks under saddle skin.

It wasn't obvious at first, but there was something about the features of her face, a shift like a landslide where the skin on the right side hung differently than the left— lower and more still. It was hard to tell because she was almost always smiling or talking, but her bottom lip, when her mouth was closed, drooped a little. She was self-conscious about it; it was why she no longer wore lipstick. That and it was so hard to put on well. But when she spoke or when she smiled, it was very hard to tell. Mina had remembered that Jake was coming. She said she left herself a little note just in case and asked the nurse, who had been with her that day when he called, to remind her as well. But she had remembered.

"It has been years and years since I heard from your father. How is he?"

It occurred to Jake that he had expected her to know, but of course there was no reason she would. "He passed away, actually, a few months ago."

Mina reached towards him, her hand feather-light on his knee. "Poor boy, I'm sorry." She looked at the pictures on her walls, "I remember when your mother died. You were so young then."

Asking if he could show her something, Jake pulled her pristine envelope out of his pocket. "I found it among my father's things." She held it out at arm's length at first, searching with her right hand for reading glasses that were somewhere on the cluttered table beside her. Mina looked at the address on the envelope and removed the letter, her eyes moving slowly back and forth across the page.

"This was when I found him, your father." Mina flipped the envelope over in her hand. "Or rather how I came across him again." She told Jake about a birth announcement in the national newspaper. "So I fibbed a little. I wasn't sure right at first. But your name, his name, your grandparents. I had to cut out the clipping. It took me a few days before I wrote him...before I thought I was sure."

Mr. Isaac Langley and his wife, Rose, welcome their first son, Jacob George. The boy is only grandson to Mordecai and Lillian, and Aladar and Malka, all deceased.

"He told me it was your mother's idea. She asked him to put it in both the national and the local papers. She was so excited." Mina rested the envelope on the plush arm of her chair. "I was worried at first to write but I thought, if I am wrong, the letter will just be sent back or thrown away."

"But you were right? You knew my father?"

"Oh, I did, very well." The borders of her irises were hazy and the whites of her eyes yellow, as if the colour had seeped and muddied the rest — but they shone, a glossy film catching the dim light cast from a tableside lamp. If it wasn't so cluttered, the room would have felt very cold even in the middle of the afternoon. Mina tugged at the peach knit throw that sat beneath her, pulling the ends up over the tops of her thighs. "Isaac was my friend. He met me when I was a girl."

"How did you meet?"

"They stayed a while with my family."

"They?"

"He and his uncle. For a short time only."

"What was my father like then?"

"Oh," she smiled, yanking gently on the sleeve of her blouse, the cuff slipping over her wrist into the palm of her hand. "He was so smart. A little shy, though he didn't think so. And sweet." Mina let her head rest in the corner of her chair. "I remember, it was the time, we were rarely alone but we did get to go out together when he was helping me watch my brothers. Isaac always made sure to walk on the outside of the sidewalk so that if there was any mud from the road or a missing plank of wood, his boots would get dirty and not mine. Every time."

"So he was a gentleman."

"Exactly." Cocking her head forward, dragging out the syllables for emphasis, "A *real* gentleman because he hadn't been taught."

Mina pointed to a black and white picture of an elderly gentleman on her dresser. "My father was very fond of him and of his uncle. He thought maybe he could inspire one of my brothers to be a scholar." Weary, she turned to smile at Jake but there was nothing in it for him, the stretch of her lips and her face stiff. "It was a hard time."

She hadn't known that Ike would run. When it was her turn, one of her brothers tried to make her run, too. "Not too long after Isaac left, my father and my brothers made a plan.

They sent me, my mother, and my sisters to Warsaw to live with relatives who had money. My father thought it would be safer. We thought what could happen to women?"

Mina pointed to a picture sitting in a small frame on the side table. It was a young boy in a sailor cap riding a toy wooden horse and laughing so hard he looked about to fall off.

"Before we left," she said, "my brother told me to remember that I could look like them. I should be a tall blonde."

Jake looked at her sitting before him, her diminutive form. An old woman, a survivor, a great-grandmother, and she looked more like a child sitting in a grown-up's chair than anything resembling a tall blonde. His stare brought Mina back to herself. She smiled at him again, "It is hard to tell now but I was quite tall. Almost 5'5. But always dark like my mother. Still, I told myself every day, you are tall and fair, with light eyes just like them. When I walked down the street, I would repeat the thought over and over again in my head. One time, when I caught a glimpse of my own reflection in a window, it startled me. My brown eyes...my brown hair was still there." She reached up and stroked the fluff of hair that sat at the nape of her neck, keeping her hand there, posed. "The only thing yellow about me was the patch on my sleeve. I had thought it was working." Falling away, her hand drifted to back to the envelope. "No one else was fooled."

They chatted a little while about her family — Mina guiding the conversation and Jake following along as her thoughts wound this way and that. At one point, Jake excused himself to her tiny washroom. Cupping his hands in the shell-shaped sink, he counted the row of perfume bottles lining the back of the counter. He hadn't noticed before but both she and the room smelled like a woman — a young, not an old, woman.

When he returned to his seat, Mina had brought the envelope to her lap. "Did you know your father was the first boy I ever had feelings for?" She kicked her foot out in front of her, the high pitch of her laugh hanging in the air, her words returned to the excited timbre he had heard on the phone. "I had not thought about him in ages. Then my granddaughter had her heart broken at school. So I told her about the first boy I ever liked and how he had to leave, and I was heartbroken. I said that she too would get over it fine. My Jessica," she pointed to one of the unframed pictures on her wall, "she's going to go to school to be a doctor."

Jake got up out of his chair and moved past Mina, bending over the bed to look closer. The woman in the picture was long past school age. She was near the ocean in a bathing suit, a ten-year-old girl with wet hair clutched tight to her side.

"Where did you say Isaac was?"

Without moving, he answered her, "He passed away. Heart problems."

"Oh." Jake could hear her body shift in its seat, fabric against fabric in the chair. "In one of his letters, your mother passed away."

"Yeah, a long time ago."

"Her heart, too."

"An aneurysm."

"I remember."

Jake heard her pat the seat of his empty chair, calling him back to her. "You better watch your heart then, be careful since that kind of trouble runs in the family."

He nodded his head, easing back down by her side. "I do." Jake looked at the envelope she held in her hands. "You said letters?"

"Yes, we wrote each other for a while. Every few months, back and forth, for a while. It can take forever to catch up. I don't think we ever wrote about anything new, just sharing the news of what we each had missed." She waved the envelope he had given her like a fan. "Is this the only one?"

"The only one I found."

"I kept all of them. All my letters in a shoebox."

"You and my father had a lot of that in common."

"Did we?" Her smile was girlish, flattered. "It reminds me what I have for you." Balancing on her elbow, Mina leaned to one side of her chair, her feet shuffling on the floor for balance. Jake rose and offered her his hand, guiding her out of her seat. "I still have some of his letters."

There was an oversized bureau nestled in the corner of the room by the door, carved in at the sides, its belly swollen. The heavy oak drawers adorned with metal tassel handles. Opening the second drawer, Mina pulled out at least a dozen envelopes held together with a wide brown elastic band. "I used to have all of them like I said, but when I moved in here, well," she turned to face Jake who was now standing behind her. "Moving means making choices of what you carry and what you leave behind. I knew I still kept some. They are yours now."

"Thank you for sharing them."

"I'm not sharing. I'm giving." She pressed the bundle into his hand. "I wrote to your father a few months after my brother Aaron died. He passed away not long after you were born. Isaac said that if he had known, he would have wanted to come to the funeral. I told him I would not have wanted him there. It was better just to let Aaron go." Jake spoke his condolences but regretted it immediately. Something in the way her body moved, twisted uneasily as she shook her head.

"He wasn't well for a long time. He never got better after. The letter might be in there. I'm not sure which ones I thought to keep."

He made a mental note to check the folder. To add Aaron, or rather to cross him off if his father hadn't already done so. It was then Jake noticed the original envelope still in her hand. Mina laid it purposefully into his palm on top of the others. "Isaac was always very tender."

She called Ike tender, but Jake couldn't help but to remember. All the times they heard his mother crying, the way her voice would sound coming through the wall of her room. Rose used to cry with the door open. The little boy thought how strange it was, how when he would cry it would be into his pillow, muffled. Rose used to cry into the open room, neither quiet nor loud, but hard, with the force of her entire body until she was too tired, until all her sound died away into silent shaking. It happened often that she would start with him

165

standing there, somewhere nearby in the room, how he would disappear to her, watching her even though she could no longer see him. He remembered how other times he would just peek in to see her sitting there, and how Ike never looked — only stood with his eyes closed, back leaned against the wall in the hallway, out of view. Then how his father would disappear into the basement, coming out only after Rose had grown silent and still, as if even from down there he knew it was over. Jake had learned to walk away.

"To be honest, that's not really how I remember my father."

"Well, you knew the man. I knew the boy." Again, Mina reached for him, finding his elbow under his sleeve, letting her hand rest there, dimly clutching the fabric. "Don't be too hard on him." Jake followed her gaze as it sank down from his face, resting focused somewhere in the middle of his chest. "We cannot know how the people we love were changed. Only see the cracks in them." She was thinking of someone, someone else. He wasn't sure; he thought he saw it in her face. "Some people are just too badly broken to ever be put back together again. Too many of the little pieces are lost along the way." Mina wanted to tell Jake that it is a squandering of spirit to long for what might have, could have, should have been yours. She wanted to but she had grown tired, and she felt one of her tremors growing in the flesh of her cheek.

Jake squeezed her tight when he said goodbye. They had both expected, had wanted, his visit to last longer but the effort of it had worn Mina out.

Despite his original plan to spend the night in Toronto, Jake traced his route back directly from the retirement residence to the highway. He had wanted to ask her about the papers, the *shemot*. He hadn't been prepared to hear what she had to say about his father, the young shy gentleman, and so in the moment, all he wanted was to go home. Restless, alert, he slid the letters into the side of the car door where they sat on top of misplaced pen caps and rolled-up gum wrappers. With each stop for gas or a coffee break, he would feel for them there, groping, checking with his car door still swung open before drifting back onto the highway.

———————

He didn't know it yet, but Jake would learn of the things that should have been when he read his father's letters. Of the babies his mother tried and tried to have. Of the third miscarriage when she, despite tradition and superstition, named the foetus inside of her hoping it would help, that God would not take from her what she could already call by name. How Aaron, like Rose, had left Europe with scarladen insides. How that other baby had been "Jacob" also.

פִּדְיוֹן הַבֵּן

REDEMPTION OF THE
FIRST BORN

§

Shevat 5699

February 1939

For the first night in weeks, I do not wake to the sound
of Uncle's heavy breathing beside me; his eyes half-
closed, neck bent forward, caught between sleep and
waking, sitting up in a chair he has pulled to be close to
me. To keep watch. I had gotten used to his rhythm while
I lay, also caught somewhere short of resting, coated in
sticky sheets of sweat, pinned to beds in different places.
One night, two nights at most, and then moving on,
though the fever stuck with me, and it would have been
better for us to stay in one place. Uncle explained to me
while we rode out of another shtetl this morning with
me wrapped in blankets and spread out across the
wagon's wooden floor. "There is no time, we must keep
moving." He wiped my head with the yellow-stained
handkerchief he now keeps in his vest for just that purpose. "If you can keep your eyes open, I will point out to
you the place where we got our name." But I didn't and
now I am in a home somewhere; I am in a real bed and
Uncle is not in the room. The silence created by his ab-
sence has shaken me out of a deep sleep.

For the first night in weeks, I wake up and my mind

is clear, my forehead and body cool. Scanning the room without lifting my head, I spy a bent knee, a small hill beyond the horizon of my covers. Uncle is not here, but I am not alone.

Trying to speak, a gurgle escapes in the place of words. My throat tightens and I must roll onto my chest to stop the coughing. "Careful, careful. Do not force anything." Zalman's voice approaches me from the foot of the bed. The coughing fit has brought the return of my headache; my throat releases and that pain is replaced by pounding behind my eyes. I moan and stretch out on my back. Zalman is sitting up, his arms crossed and resting on my bed. His face is worried, his dark messy eyebrows pushed down into a flat line. "If you force it, your body will never heal. Not all the way. And you'll need that."

"Where's my uncle?" The words come out shallow and sore.

"He is asleep in his own room. He's been sitting up with you for almost three weeks...he's been so worried. Earlier, though, he could see the fever had broken and so I convinced him to get some rest while I looked after you." Zalman rubs his chin through the bristles in his beard. He is not yet fourteen, younger than me, but he is already everywhere covered in hair. "I think he only agreed to it because we're here. He's home."

"Here?"

"Kutno. The end."

"He's home?"

"It's what he said when we arrived. We're at your cousin's. The rabbi said I could stay here, with you, until you got better and left town. Your uncle thought it was a great idea. If only they knew, huh, Izzy."

Nodding my head is like swinging a lead weight, backwards and forwards, inside my skull. "Right Zeama, if only they knew."

———

Narrow and tall, Zalman was the darkest of the four boys that moved with us across Poland on our way to Kutno. Heinach, Laib, Menachem, and Zalman. The other three were brothers and spoke mainly to each other. Zalman spoke to me. He was not as shy as the other boys. He read newspapers and periodicals that his father and brothers would collect along their route to and from the markets in the larger cities: *Maly Przeglad, Yiddish Telegraten Agentur, Nasz Kurier.* Zalman said his father picked up whatever writing he could find in Yiddish, spent money on papers from all across the country, and brought them home for his youngest son to read.

Zalman said his father often brought home papers in German, and he would have one of the *volksdeutch* from the market translate what Zalman could not decipher for himself. He spoke of cartoons he had seen that were in French. They were not the kind for children. These cartoons were about soldiers with large muddy boots. Or pigs dressed in fancy vests with gold jewellery. One was a man with a crooked nose clutching the world in two sharp, dirty fists...fists and hooves. Zalman told me about these cartoons when we travelled at night while the others were asleep. He had said he understood them without knowing the meaning of the words. I understood them, too. He stopped describing them to me when, early in my fever, I cried out to my uncle about the men in their heavy black boots surrounding me. He stopped talking about these things entirely, afraid, he said, that I might accidentally reveal something more. He said he was also afraid these thoughts were making me sicker. I will never tell him but those nights, his voice narrated some of my most horrible dreams. The others were about Aaron.

Tonight he tells me how he had waited, watching Uncle watching me, praying for me to get better.

———

The Kutno *shtiebel* is flanked on two sides by cemetery. Uncle tells me our people have been here for almost five centuries, and at the beginning, the cemetery marked the boundaries of the shtetl. Over time, the shtetl grew in size, spilling out beyond the cemetery, encompassing it so that the *shtiebel* and the shul would remain in the centre. Now the cemetery sits like two eyes peering out from the heart of Kutno. Or sentinels. Dead spaces, which cushion the shul on either side.

"We passed the road which stretches south to Lodz on our way here." Uncle walks with me to the shul, making sure I keep my body guarded from the wind, the houses on my left and his body on my right as shields. My cousin, my uncle's cousin, has given me three mufflers to wear and two pairs of mitts. Only my eyes and mouth know that it is still winter. I begged Uncle to let me come today, get out of bed and keep him company. I have been so useless to him for so long, being only another thing for him to worry about. Surely today as I am back to normal I can be of some help. We still have our work to do.

Looking up as I walk, clotheslines lattice the air between the buildings and cut the light blue of the morning sky. It is still winter but the worst has passed and spring is soon to follow. Hints of this passing of time, time which I have missed, appear as drops of melting ice that rib the white strings which hang over my head.

Uncle passes through the low gate by the synagogue and holds it open behind him for me to follow. Now I have no buildings nearby to block the wind, and its full force seems to hit my exposed skin all at once. "I wanted to tell you a story then. About Lodz, do you remember?" Opening my mouth, I let out hot air which carries my reply, "Yes," and then quickly press my mittened hands to my lips in order to keep any more warmth from escaping.

"You have to know where a name comes from if you

want to know where something — where you — come from." He must be noticing that I am holding my face because he stops and looks back quickly at the way we have come and then forward to the distance to where we are going, as if measuring if it is better to move forward or to turn back. I let my hands drop down to my sides, signalling to him that I feel okay. I would sooner get sick all over again than be sent back, stuck in bed away from him.

"Tell me the story," I say and continue down our path towards the shul.

For a moment, Uncle remains standing there and then with a shrug he carries on behind me, "It is a long story. Perhaps I will wait until we are inside."

"The world, or at least our place in it, this place, has not changed very much over time. Generations ago, there were pogroms just as there are now. Sometimes, in some of the larger communities, word would get out, rumours of what was about to come — like the lightning before thunder.

"In one such community, there was a Jewish merchant who worked as an agent for one of the powerful Polish politicians. He heard things, saw the lightning bolts streak the sky. And so he went to the Polish community, the police, and people in the street, and made them an offer. He would give one gold coin for every live unharmed Jewish person who was brought to him during the pogrom. More than that, he would give one silver coin for every dead Jewish body brought to him unharmed. The goyim must have thought he was crazy. It was dangerous: they could have come to his house instead, robbed him, killed him and taken his money. Of course, they wouldn't — his powerful connection with Polish authority meant he was to be spared from harm. So he stood amongst them and repeated his offer.

"The next night, the shtetl was razed, absorbed by the lapping tongues of flames. People were beaten and killed. The merchant watched this torrent around him, waiting, and soon enough Polish men began arriving at his door. At first, he was handing out mainly silver coins but as they saw that he was holding true to his deal, more and more of the living were brought to his door. Hundreds and hundreds were saved. And those who were not could at least be buried and put at peace. After that day he was called by a new last name. Langlebben. Long life. It was given to him as a blessing from the community that he saved. And now that last name is yours."

Uncle's hand is open, his palm turned upwards. In it, he weighs hundreds of imaginary coins, hundreds of lives. I see their invisible load fill his hand. I watch it sway up and down between us. While he speaks, I focus on his hand, shakier than I remember, the skin years older even than it seemed mere weeks ago. I avoid his eyes.

The shul is busy: boys and men passing us on all sides, tables covered in open books, the low whispering of voices in study. In this place, Kutno, there are many men like Uncle, learned like him. Half of my mind listens to his story and the other half... the other half is possessed by that word: lightning. A part of my mind stays stuck on that single idea, the power of it. It as if he has read my thoughts, some of them, the ones Zalman was so worried I'd share. Or let slip. I search for the lesson in this history, hoping, hoping I am understanding it right.

"To know what something is, you must know what its name means. If you know where a name comes from, you can know where you come from. We look back to know in which direction to face forward." Uncle curls his hand into a fist and sets it down with a soft tap on the table between us. "You are one in a line of many, Yitzhak, the name you carry has been carried to you by others and now it is yours to carry forward. This name is a link in a chain."

"If pogroms happen, again and again as often as you say they do, what are we doing here? If it was just another pogrom? And if it's not..." I cannot finish my thought. I know he would be too angry.

He opens his mouth to answer but the sound is drowned out by a loud *thud* which echoes off the walls of the shul. A book has been knocked off a table to the floor. The men rush over, including Uncle, who moves instinctively out of his seat, to examine what book has fallen. The boy whose elbow has caused the disruption sits pale, stiff in his seat, himself unsure of what he has done. The cantor, a friend of my uncle's, kneels down over the splayed pages. He nudges my uncle who peers over his shoulder and together they begin to laugh in relief. The boy is too surprised to react. No doubt he can hardly believe his luck. With all the holy and prayer books on the table, his clumsiness has sent flying nothing more important than book of children's stories and an exercise book full of his own scribblings.

The cantor rises to his feet, slapping the boy's knee on his way. He and Uncle chuckle together, leaning into one another as if telling secrets. The boy, now more embarrassed than frightened, buries his head in his hands as his friends crowd around the table, laughing and teasing. It is terrible, I think, that Uncle and the cantor should laugh at him until I realize that the boy is laughing too, his feet swinging happily underneath the table. Slowly everyone returns to their work and Uncle, back at my side, suggests we make our way home for lunch. With his words, I notice how stuffy the room has become, the air warm and musty. My feverish dizziness threatens its return in the back of my head.

"Yes," I say, "I think I have had enough for today."

And if it's not, why are we spending time saving she-mot from burning but not the people?

I know tonight that when I try to sleep, again I will

have nightmares about Aaron. I had hoped they would go with the fever, but now thinking straight, they are worse. There are more of them. In every one, I am there, she is there, and I wake only after I have been pushed in the snow. I must bite my tongue because always I wake with the taste of blood in my mouth.

———

Betrayal and guilt are heavy solids: hard to swallow and they just sit there like blistering stones in the hollow of your stomach, hard to digest.

The face in the bathroom mirror is the same; there is no outward way to tell. The change does not show in the skin, and I thank God for it. It would be too much.

Days pass and I remain light-headed, moody, rocked by nights of fitful sleep. Zalman is given leave to stay with me longer, as I am clearly not yet well. Uncle's worry only makes it worse, prolongs this restlessness. Before I would have spoken to him about it as I always have, I would feel more certain if I could speak up now. I know, however, without speaking what he would say. Besides, I know he wouldn't listen, not to all of it, and this waiting and biding time would only be harder.

Now the attention Uncle pays me is embarrassing. I hide in my bedroom and ask that he no longer sleep beside me; I tell him that at night I would prefer Zalman's company. Zalman talks to me at night like he did on our trip here of stories he has read, rumours he has heard.

Tonight, he tells me about Eli, his neighbour, who over a year ago banged on every door in the shtetl, screaming about his daughter who lived in Berlin, begging people to give him money to help her move home. When asked why, he would just mumble over and over again that something has happened, "something has happened." He says his father made him go into the street, to watch Eli panic, trying to find anyone who would listen. Zalman talks on, but I cannot get over that the man thought he could save his daughter by bringing her back *here*.

"Why, Zeama?" I let my voice interrupt his speech, "Why did your father make you pay attention to such things?" But I know the answer; why he was sent here, so unlike the other boys, with both winter and summer clothes in his bag. Zalman knows he need not answer, so merely picks up his story where he left off, talking at me until he is finished. "Something is happening, Izzy, and you and I know it. My father knew it and that's why he told me to go. Your uncle knows it, too."

I cannot sleep at all now. The two of us lie together awake in my room. I recognize this feeling as being homesick but cannot share it with Zalman; he'd think I was a baby, though he is younger than me. Maybe he'd leave me behind. It is something I must get used to. At least it will be something familiar.

Again I pray that my face does not change and stays frozen just like this. I look, have always looked, just like my father. I will have my face instead of a photograph. But I know already that is too much to ask. *We cannot be the same people in two different lives.*

"Kutno is the closest I will ever again be to home." Zalman does not answer, but I'm sure he has heard me. *Fine, we will both pretend to sleep.*

———

"Yitzhak, I have asked you twice." Stolen out of a daydream, I turn to look at my uncle sitting beside me at the table. "Please pass me the butter."

Using only my fingertips, I pick up the cold dish and move it carefully, passing over my own breakfast plate before laying it down in front of him. My cousin's husband, who sits across from me, chews his hard bread by grinding it down between his teeth. I watch his lower jaw slide, pushing his chin out, back and forth. When he speaks, the soggy slop in his mouth slaps against the roof of his mouth, "You've been increasingly distracted these days." He looks down at my full plate: one large crust of bread and a cup of vegetable broth his wife has made especially for the invalid.

She nudges my plate across the table, pushing its rim up against the edge of the table and causing the pale green to slosh dangerously around the bowl's lip. "Nonsense, poor thing hasn't been sleeping at all. I can hear him shifting around in his room all night."

Uncle's cousin and her husband look very much

alike. They both have large foreheads defined by thick, dark eyebrows. He is bald except for a trim of shiny curls which stretches around his head from ear to ear and up around his crown. Her *babushkah* sits so low that it is impossible to see if she has any hair at all, and with their faces so much the same, it is easier to picture her with nothing but the same curly patches. The only difference is her blue eyes. Zalman told me he thinks that means she was probably very beautiful when she was younger before she was married. That is because everything about a woman can change but her eyes. They are just like Uncle's.

Despite myself, I am indeed quite hungry. Cupping the bowl in one palm, I begin scooping the soup quickly into my mouth. My cousin looks pleased. Later, when Zalman teases me about my appetite returning, I will tell him I ate it for her. Now that I appear back to normal, Uncle can go back to eating his own meal.

"I was thinking of going into the market today," he says after clearing his plate. Pushing the now empty bowl away, I pick up the bread in both of my hands and try to pull it apart.

Flakes of crust fall from my hands into my lap, "I'll go with you. I'd like to get out and stretch my legs." Uncle turns, his face does its best to mask surprise. I pretend not to notice him out of the corner of my eye. Instead, I wring the bread in my hands, working its fibres apart.

"I'd like that," he says finally and returns his attention to his mug. I shrug and shove a wad of the bread's dry innards into my mouth.

———

Crouching over, Zalman leans his elbows on the frame of my chair, reading over my shoulder. He is close enough for me to feel the scratch of his beard and *peyas* brush the top of my ear. At first, I tried to block his view by hunching my right shoulder down and writing with my elbow pushed way out to the side. But my handwriting is already so jerky, the letters slippery on the page, that I stop.

Repositioning my arm, I move the pencil slowly, pressing its lead tip hard into the paper. Uncle has to be able to read this. I have to be able to read this; perhaps the letter will be able to convince us both. Standing, stretching to his full height, Zalman tries to shake my chair, jerking a couple of times on its frame. "We are doing what is best for everyone. It would be impossible to take them with us, and we can do no good for them, or anyone, here. You'll see, Izzy, you'll see." He uses his hand to pat me reassuringly on the back, but it doesn't work. One, two, the palm of his hand lands on my back just a little too hard.

All this time, talking of plans, and I never once agreed out loud to go. But then, I never once argued... never once said I wouldn't, or that I would stay. Even now, there is no need for me to say anything. If Zalman wants to believe we will ever be back here, it is better for him. I tried my best to say goodbye today, but it was harder than I expected. He doesn't understand why I am bothering to leave anything at all—a note if not an explanation. *I cannot,* I think, *go without saying goodbye. He will need something to give to my mother.* "They will know we did the right thing," he says.

"I don't think my family will know why I am doing it at all."

Zalman sighs through his nose, a sound I have grown accustomed to already. It is reserved for his frustration with me and different from the noises he makes for the rest of the world. "We will go somewhere different. Where we can be safe to do something. Somewhere far enough away where none of this is happening."

"No Zeama, maybe we can outrun the rain but never the storm."

Dear Uncle,

> *I looked up and saw the break of light in the sky.*
> *Your Yitzhak L.*

§

When the plane met the gate, it was already two hours past sunrise. The peel of light from the open door stung Jake's eyes, harder than the amber glow that he had felt come through the panel of oval windows. He had expected the city to hold that colour: the goldish yellow so beautifully photo-graphed and displayed in so many pictures. But the sun here, untempered by the glass of a camera's lens or an airplane's plastic, was pure white light and everything in the city —or the airport, at least— stood out in sharp relief against the April sky. It did not glow like he had expected.

Jake realized that part of it was having spent the better portion of the last nine hours awake with only his overhead light keeping him from near total darkness. Having climbed from the runway during the last moments of dusk, Jake had na-ively anticipated that the cabin would be lit by the usual soft night-lighting he remembered from previous trips. Not so on Royal Air Maroc. After dinner was served, the overhead lights were switched off and the cabin was allowed to go completely dark. There wasn't even a twinkling runway up and down the aisle to guide his way from the bathroom back into his seat. When the over-the-ocean movie came on and the rest of the passengers were lit up by the shifting colours of every scene, Jake saw nothing. A loose monitor directly in front of him left Jake's row and the two rows behind him with only the audio of the film available to them through too-large earphones.

He had had no plans to watch the movie anyway, even if it hadn't been one he'd seen before about a magical boy whose parents had also died and left him full of questions. Instead, as soon as his tray was cleared, Jake pulled out his papers and tried to write. To put it all together. He started with a name. His father's. He wrote it out just as he had seen, as he had put on the form himself. Now in his notepad, he tried to start the story, put some shape to it, the same kind he had been able to put to the others—to Chaim, and Mina, and Ida. But again and again, he hit the same blank space. Instead, of writing, he settled for sleeplessness, looking into a night sky lit by the intermittent flashing of the lights on the plane's wing.

Jake's seat was just behind the barrier that held business back from first class, only several rows ahead of another makeshift divider behind which coach loomed. Seda had encouraged him to use the money from his father's estate sale to purchase the middle-grade ticket and Jake was grateful for it, his knees almost buckling as, upon landing, he had bounded for the front of the plane and down the steps onto the tarmac.

––––––––––

It was late morning when Jake arrived at the old man's house in the downtown mellah.

"I have some things I want to take you to." They were the first words out of Zalman's mouth, uttered at the same time the groggy-eyed traveller crossed the threshold of his home. Though Jake spoke French well enough, his hosts used English to save him the effort of translation.

Erika, Zalman's better half, reached to take the handle of the rolling suitcase from Jake, shushing her husband. "Rest first, then you two can spend the day." Her fingers on his forearm, guiding him into the spare room, were the only cool thing he had felt since stepping off the plane. The sun had yet to reach its apex in the sky and already the temperature was almost thirty-five degrees. The metal rails of the seats on the train he took into the city had been hot and sticky, body heat and sweat infusing around him, and the air in the taxi he took from the station was even worse. Before knocking, Jake had inadvertently smelled his hand, the history of every odour from the cab's interior stuck in the grooves of his skin.

When facing him, Erika had to tip her head back, but only slightly, to look Jake straight in the eye. With a metronome's precision, the click of her high heels, perfectly paced, guided him down the tile hallway: heel, ball, heel, ball.

Unlike everything he had expected, Erika still had all the thick black hair of her youth, only here and there strands lightened either by the sun or by age, worn swept up in a bun that clung messily off-centre on the back of her head. Younger than her husband, only just approaching her seventies, Erika's angular features — sharp nose, sharp chin, thin mouth — pulled the shape of her face down from a wide forehead into a heart. Her skin matched the deep tan of her husband, though hers was obviously a natural umber.

The room to which Jake was led and left to rest, a sofa bed already pulled out with tucked sheets, must have usually served as Zalman's office. The room held the smell of years of cigar and cigarette smoke, Zalman's arthritis having long ago forced him to give up his pipe, being too hard to pack and too tricky to light.

On a sideboard pushed against the wall to make room for the guest, was a framed wedding photo of the Weisses. A late twenties-something Zalman, his European skin pink from the sun, was smiling beside his young Spanish bride. The couple was seated in a huddle of Erika's family — mostly her father's side, Spanish Jews who had emigrated to the country generations earlier. Erika's mother, who looked more like Zalman and stood with her hand pressed warmly on his shoulder, had been Bulgarian before moving to Morocco fewer than three decades before. That was how such a European name came to be hung on such a Spanish mantle.

Left alone in the room, curtains drawn, Jake lay down and considered sleep. Overtired and hot, instead he let himself daydream, kept company by the now familiar voices of Zalman and Erika that would drift his way down the hall and the occasional bark or whimper of the dogs he had seen sunbathing outside. He must have dozed off at some point though, for he had not noticed the several times Erika had checked in on him — first pressing her ear to the closed door to listen, then opening it a crack to make sure with her eyes that he was okay. It was only the sound of a late lunch being spread on a table that fully roused him and got him out of bed.

Straightening the collar on his black polo shirt, he sat at the table, "I'm sorry I was out for so long. I guess I didn't realize how exhausting the trip was."

Zalman sat across from him, excited, smiling. He pushed a glass full of ice water over to Jake, "You will eat and then we will go see."

———

Together they pushed their way through the crowd at the Casablanca-Voyageurs train station, the main station at the hub of the city. Zalman had told Jake that they could have kept travelling south by train, but this would be the most reliable place to find a taxi; they wouldn't have to walk too far which was good, as there would be enough walking later. Sitting side by side in the back seat, Zalman pointed to the other cars that shared the street. Some were beautiful, shiny, clean luxury vehicles, buffed vessels, here and there steered by professional drivers. These moved in traffic alongside the other vehicles that looked less like cars and more like rotting mechanical corpses, innards hanging out of dented hoods, fumes rising from both the back and front ends.

"Fez, the city where Izzy and I first lived here, still you see donkeys in the roads. Even here, every rare time, a donkey."

Jake tugged at the moist armpits of his shirt, doing his best to keep the fabric away from his skin. "That's the way it works. Even in the same country, one place takes two steps forward, the other stays two steps back."

"True, true." Zalman eyed Jake admiringly, "Places and people, too."

The round-stone paved streets of the mellah of Azemmour were drizzled with green Northern stars, the leaves off the trees that lined the main paths through the area. In the cab, Zalman had explained that "mellah" came from *melh,* the Arabic word for salt. Jake wondered how the name came to be used for the Jewish quarter, the walled-in communities, the Islamic solution for a European ghetto. The old man just shrugged, "Perhaps it is a bitter taste. Perhaps they wish we could just melt away. Or perhaps it is just a word."

Other than the small tourist plaque liberally sprinkled with the word "*Juifs,*" nothing in empty Azemmour spoke to what the place once had been. Abandoned, home now only to a saints' shrine, all the doors had been shut and locked decades ago, keeping imaginary visitors out of vacant rooms.

Jake swept his fingers along the cool walls of buildings that they passed. Zalman, his guide, shuffled them zigzagged across streets so they remained always on the side with the most shade. The afternoon sun still high above them, they strolled with purpose along lanes and down covered alleys, all the while Zalman telling stories, for Jake and that vacant shtetl.

The narration, filled with the smells and colours that held precedence in Zalman's memory, fleshed out what Jake had already known — about the end of his father's tour of Poland and his escape, with a younger boy he called Zeama, out of Europe. The miles and miles of travel which had always been blended into broad strokes were again swept easily over: "We had to cross a border... we stayed there a little... so we left and got our way onto the boat..."

Zalman gave to Jake, instead, the minutiae — the bits and the pieces of the story beyond geography or logistics. Rather than speak in detail of a trip by foot, by train, towards Russia, the old man held fanned fingers against his temples as he recalled the first night they slept on the ground just after the border: "The taiga, swamp forest. Izzy decided it was smart to sleep under the lowest branches we found, to hide. But at morning, we could barely get up. Fallen pines and all the sap bled onto our chests and faces, over our mouths...like waking up under water, eyelids sealed closed." Wrinkled fingertips crawled across his face, picking at bygone needles and syrup. "He said to me to wet my lips, wet my lips and use the spit on my fingers to open my eyelashes."

He described how hungry they had been when they finally resorted to picking day old pastry from the bin behind the bakery in the small town north of Paris. One day, the baker caught them, screaming as they ran down the alley and into the street. How the next day, the thrown-out food had been spoiled, with dirty water and cigarette ash poured over top of it. How it meant being hungry for days again.

He described the first thing he saw when the two of them had arrived in the city of the endless mosque. "The boat stopped in Tangier, and if you followed the road, straight to Fez. We came to Bab Boujeloud. The gate looking like the entrance to a temple. Each tile was a different blue. Ocean, sky, navy, turquoise, every blue. Right away, we were afraid to go through, I did not know even if we would be allowed. Izzy waited to be told to leave. I decided what to lose so I ran through in, like the uninvited guest I was. I turned around to see if he came with me and was stunned. The whole inside of the gate was green—one green—like moss. That was when he took me, pulled me by the arm and we walked fast down into the city. 'Zeama,' he said, 'if you are going to run, do not stop. Just keep running.' I could not really help it. I missed for a long time being in a place so pretty."

As Zalman spoke, Jake pictured his father's list, crossing

out and adding names, building out the page. They had reached a courtyard at the centre of the old mellah. A magnificent spiral of layered stone wound around the edges of the courtyard, tighter and tighter, towards what once was a fountain in the middle of the open space. Nine different lanes and alleys converged on the courtyard. Zalman told Jake how after only a few weeks in Fez, he and Ike had decided to come to Azemmour, a bigger community of Jews where they could find a better place to live and maybe earn a living.

"I liked Azemmour better than Fez, everything crowded— but not by strangers." He spread his hands, gesturing to the open space around, "By other people like us. Your father thought we should stay in the bigger city, but eventually he gave in."

"Safety in numbers."

"For me maybe. For your father, never. Never safe enough." Without hesitation, Zalman turned down the third alley to the left of where they had entered. He had not come there in years but his body, his legs, remembered every path, every shortcut. "We were shtetl boys, all of what we knew, so I found us a new shtetl."

The alley was short, spilling back onto a larger street, one Jake had not seen before. "Together we lived in an apartment. This was all stores with apartment on top." Jake had given into the heat. Dazed, he let his mind and body trail gingerly behind Zalman, following behind the sound of his words, the sound of his feet as rubber soles padded across the ground. "It was not the same for him here as for me. I found my place here, so I stopped running. Izzy had further to go, always running. I am not sure he ever really stopped."

Using his foot to kick open a rusted iron gate, Zalman shepherded the young man down stone steps into a private lane with an arched ceiling. Down, away from the street, guarded by a rotten fence which held the wayward leaves away, Jake noticed how easily his rubber sandals slid over the old stone, rubbed sleek over time. The far end of the lane was uncovered, sunlight dropping through branches stretched across its width. Zalman pointed to the white wood slat door in front of them, "I met Erika here. The backdoor to her father's house." Jake reached out to where the handle must once have been, his knuckles grazing a gentle rap on the wood. "I married her in there, too. And we lived with all her family until we left."

Turning, leaving their patch of sunlight to make their way back to the street, Zalman told Jake how he and Erika, like most of the Jews, left Morocco. He talked about how as a boy he had always wanted to study languages, how even though the only school he had known was a religious one, he imagined what it would be like to go to university — something, he lamented, Orthodox Jews like him didn't really do. But he was good at languages, learning French better and faster than Izzy, the logic of the vernacular always evident and sensible to him. And Erika's father—how he had been Zalman's inspiration.

"He would have been a professor but it was not possible here. He was a math tutor. All of his children were good at maths." It would be best for them to find somewhere else to be. And so Zalman and Erika, funded by her father, moved to France where he could go to school, and she could work in one of the shops. "I studied everything. English, French, Russian, everything. Later, German too."

Zalman was an etymologist. Jake remembered Rose had told him when he was a kid — how words grew like children do and how Uncle Zalman knew the birth of every word, its parents, aunts and uncles, everything. Or how a multitude of different words could all be borne from the same single seed word. Syllables and prefixes like plants and children.

The couple had been happy there for a long time. "France was good to us." His hand on Jake's shoulder, guiding him to steer left even though the street swerved right. "Always good to us until it was no longer good."

If you were to ask Zalman, he would tell you that the word "diaspora" came from the Greek and meant to scatter about or disperse: "A place where we must carry our history on our backs because there is nowhere to put it down." If, perchance, you were to ask Zalman while his wife was in the room, Erika would hold her head still, watching her husband flip through the information in his mind, delving for the path, the history of the word. Then she would lean closer to where you sat on the couch or in a chair. "If you had asked me, I would say it sounds more like 'disappear.'"

A fork in the road brought the men out of the old mellah and back onto a busy street. Zalman pointed down the block, at a half-moon driveway under a large striped red and white canopy, "The hotel. We can go there to get a taxi." Jake eased his pace to match the old man whose usual stride had been slowed by uneven stones and avenues connected by stairways. Jake signalled for a taxi while Zalman rested. Sitting on a carved bench in front of the hotel, Zalman rubbed his hip as he spoke. "Erika wanted to come home. It was time. Her family is still here. I had no reason to argue. France was no more a home for me than here, so we came back."

Jake stood close behind him as Zalman clambered into the back of the taxi, his arms open, tentative and waiting, should they be needed. But Zalman got in just fine on his own. He reached and grabbed the handle of the other door, pulling himself over to the far end of the seat to make room for Jake who climbed in after.

After giving the driver directions in French, Zalman leaned into Jake and spoke more quietly, "It is not so great for us here. The reason your father said he would never come back to visit. I told him here it was dangerous maybe, but there," he said, a cocked finger poking Jake hard in the chest, "it was cold." The old man shrugged and moved back to his side of the seat. "Last year, after the bombs, he called me. He said after Poland, and Russia, and France, everywhere we were not wanted, he asked what I thought to do. If I was scared." Zalman frowned, the damp pink flesh of his inside lower lip rolling out beyond his top lip's reach. "I told him not anymore." Zalman turned to Jake, "I'm old, what is there to be scared for? Not anymore." He turned his head back to centre. "But your father, he was always scared, even of ghosts."

Jake felt the muscles wrapped around his Adam's apple

tighten. He focused hard to swallow. "It's not fair." He swallowed again, "That you talk about it, but he never bothered to say anything. Not to my mother, not to me. Never even tried."

Zalman kept his eyes fixed on the back of the cab driver's head. "It is different. It is the difference between being pushed from a train and choosing to jump."

For the rest of the ride back to Rue Verlet Hanus, neither man spoke. Instead, they let the racket of the streets near sundown pass through the taxi's open windows and fill the air around them.

———————

The first time Zalman came to Canada, it had been for Rose's funeral. Ike had known better than to try to stop him. The truth was that though he could never ask, Ike wanted him there. For the first time since he had met his wife, he felt truly alone again. Like he had when they were young.

At the cemetery, everyone took turns piling dirt onto her coffin. Respectful, they nodded at Ike when their turn had passed and made their ways back to the cars parked along the cemetery's main road. The two men stood there until everyone had left. The two men on one side, a young boy, eleven years old on the other. Zalman stood there a long time, watching Jake and holding his oldest friend's hand. It was Ike who broke the silence.

"What if you get the chance to save one person in your lifetime. And what if you wasted it on yourself?"

Zalman said nothing. He just squeezed his friend's hand

harder and watched as the little boy stood crying, his knuckles white and clenched around the small shovel in his hand.

––––––––

He spread his things out on a table in the living room. Jake noticed the phone sitting on a side table by the window. It was the only phone he had spotted except for one in the kitchen. He pictured Zalman standing there, looking out, the way he must have been all those times over the years when he spoke to Ike, and then later when increasingly Jake found himself on the end of the line. It was so different now — the two of them in the same room, Zalman sitting at the table across from him.

Erika moved through the room around them, turning on lamps and adjusting the curtains so the light would be just right. She had let Jake sleep late into the day, her own morning spent readying the kitchen. It was one of those traditions Erika liked and chose to keep: sweeping away every crumb of bread, hunting every morsel out of every corner with a feather duster. Zalman had reminded her once that the real tradition was to use just one single feather.

"But," she replied, "that was not how my mother did it. And I follow her tradition, not your silly one." By the time Jake had showered and gotten dressed, the whole house smelled like the makings of the Passover Seder, every dish and preparation well on its way. The first night would be celebrated just by the three of them. Tomorrow, after Seda arrived and they picked her up from the airport, they would all go and have the second Seder at Erika's niece's house with more than a dozen other relatives and guests. Jake had asked Seda to give him time alone with Zalman, but he wanted her to be there for Passover—for the second night.

Zalman had explained the whole ritual to Seda over the phone: in Israel, Passover is observed with only the single seder. It is only in the Diaspora that many Jews perform two. "Out here, we all have to do a little more. Work a little bit harder for our prayers to be heard."

Certain that the atmosphere was now exactly perfect, Erika left the two men alone and went back to her cooking.

The papers had been laid out precisely, everything arranged in the order that Jake had decided upon. This time, this last time, he was prepared. He knew what he wanted to show Zalman first, how he would tell him what he learned— the wording just so, phrased and measured, to allow Zalman an opportunity to steer his direction should he have gone wrong, to allow Jake time and space to read the old man's face, his reaction. The specific questions which had so evaded him in the previous interviews were now on the tip of his tongue, ready for the only person left Jake felt could answer them.

Zalman eyed the arrangement before him, spread out from right to left: the overstuffed beige folder cinched at its middle by a fat brown elastic, a wide transparent-green plastic folder with black accordion sides and a flap sealed by a Velcro tab, used to transport everything, and finally, a ratty brown envelope tucked over on its side. "So you said you wanted to show me everything, you meant it. This is everything?"

Jake began working the elastic band off of the folder, "I think so. I think it's everything." Tenderly, with the palm of his hand, Jake fanned out the original contents of the folder, in one smooth motion. Without looking up, Jake took the arm of the chair beside him and moved it out from the table. Knowing his mind, Zalman got up and moved around the side of the table to sit beside him. Keeping his head low, Zalman focused on the treasure now revealed to him, his eyes moving around the pages until he sat down beside Jake and the words came into view. "Whoosh."

"Yeah." Jake followed Zalman's gaze across the pages. "There's no order to it. He seems to have just picked out anything that looked like something and kept it. All sorts of stuff crammed in together. The only common thread is that trip he took with his uncle. At least that I could see."

"Izzy. His pages." His head still bent low, Zalman began picking up pieces at random, studying each before carefully placing it back down in its spot and choosing another. Jake waited but the old man said nothing.

"There's this, though," Jake said finally, directing his attention to the list on the front of the folder, his father's handwriting. A smile found itself growing large and open across the old man's face as he recognized and took in his old friend's handwriting.

In the margin, almost falling off the page, were three checkmarks in new red ink. *Mina Rosenberg, Zeama Weiss, C. P. Yanofsky.* And at the bottom of the page, also in red ink, Jake's clumsy hand (clumsy compared to his father's sweeping script) a recent entry: *Ida Plaski, Quebec City. Rivkah Zalesky, deceased.* "This is how I found people, off of this list." Zalman leaned over the table in front of him and let his fingers walk the page, stepping tentatively down each entry, the new crowded in with the old. Jake sat back in his chair. "If you can look through it, maybe more of it will ring a bell."

Zalman looked into the younger man's face, not quite a youthful version of his oldest friend. Only that same structure, perfect rectangular forehead and impossibly deep-set eyes, teased out into the shape of almonds. The rest of him was Rose, or it must have been. Zalman carefully gathered the papers back into a high pile and flipped the folder shut. "I recognize some of them, yes, and I will tell you what I remember. But I want to know from you first. What you found."

Jake moved the paper folder back to the middle of the table, placing its elastic band on top. He reached then for the green folder, pulling against the Velcro which held the crease in the plastic shut. "Seda thought I should start a folder of my own. To keep things straight." Everything here was in order, ready to share with Zalman. Quickly skipping over the dead ends, updated obituaries and false starts, Jake focused his attention on the top of the pile, where Chaim's letter to the editor sat with a paperclip that held the scrap of paper on which he had written the man's phone number and address, as well as the date of their visit.

"This," Jake said, handing the scrap to Zalman, "is Chaim, but my father called him Pietka. They met right at the beginning of his trip." He told Zalman about the stocky old man, about everything he had said, how he had described his father, "that boy." Jake recalled how just before he left, Chaim had told him that even recently, even days before Jake's phone call, he would "think a lot about that boy. Whether or not I would get ever to see him again. But I guess I never did."

Next, Jake unfolded the papers given to him by the woman at the museum: all of the information about Ida and her family and the complete Yom Hashoah pamphlet she had given him. He had even kept the map of the museum, much crinkled and deformed as it had stayed rolled up and shoved inside his jeans pocket for days, only rediscovered as Seda was preparing the pants for laundry. Jake opened the pamphlet and showed Zalman where Seda had circled his family, where he later had found his mother's relatives listed and circled them just the same. He had recreated his father's markings on this new pamphlet, underlining the Zalesky family and circling Rivkah's name. All of this Jake handed to Zalman and told him about meeting Ida. He called her a survivor non-survivor, "you know, not technically a 'survivor' but one anyways."

Zalman waved the pamphlet at Jake, "All of us…we were all survivors, Jake. Or else…" He unfolded the pamphlet to its full length, his nails pressed hard into the shiny paper, ten fingers holding up thousands of names. "Your father was a survivor, too."

Flustered, embarrassed under the weight of the old man's face, Jake nodded his head. "Of course, right. But you know what I mean." Zalman lifted his right hand, placing it on the back of Jake's bobbing head, stilling its motion.

The photograph, trimmed along its edges, was clipped to the brochure from the retirement residence, nicked from the front desk on his way out. Tucked between the two, Jake opened and handed over Mina's letter. "This was the letter I found in the folder." Zalman hesitated, looking to Jake, asking permission to read her words. After getting the nod to continue, Zalman took a moment to read the letter thoroughly before slipping it back into its envelope. The rest of the letters, those Mina had given him, were passed over one by one, Jake summarizing their contents even as Zalman scaled their lines.

Jake explained the woman's condition and how, despite that, she seemed to remember everything about Ike and their time together. "I suppose the older stuff is harder to forget."

"Mmm. Impossible sometimes." Zalman picked up the photograph that was still sitting on the top of the much-deflated pile. Mina happy, sitting cross-legged in a red and black bathing suit on a rocky beach, less sand than gravel. Her skin is deeply bronzed and her hair, long and wet, sits in tangled waves on her shoulders. Had the camera been closer, it might have been possible to see the goose bumps running up and down her legs. Beside her, standing with arms folded in front of a pale reedy chest was a man, almost smiling — the boy on his horse, all grown-up. "This is her?"

"It was in one of the envelopes she gave me that she'd never sent. No letter, just the photo and a note addressed to my dad. Said she wanted him to have a picture—her face to go with her name. She hadn't known before I got there that he was gone. I don't think she remembered it was in there, or she probably wouldn't have given it to me."

"Maybe no. Maybe yes." Zalman handed back the photo which Jake then placed in its paperclip hold.

Jake told Zalman of the others, too — of the hours and days spent trying to track down more names of the list. The people he called, his story spoken again and again, so many times now it seemed like he had shared it all his life, but for nothing. There were either no answers, no hints of recognition. Or tired voices, repeating their own stories of loss and family members who never made it out of Europe, whose bodies would never be claimed. He held up papers with numbers crossed out, names bracketed by question marks. "Even if they did sort of remember," he said, "I wouldn't blame any of them for not wanting to talk about it."

"Easier," Zalman nodded. "It's easier to pretend to forget. Tempting."

Jake gathered the papers back into a pile in his hands, tapping the load on the table before shoving it back into the green folder. Only one sheet of paper, turned over so that all Zalman could see was its blank backside, stayed resting in front of Jake. Zalman tapped the paper. "And this?"

Jake looked neither at the old man or his finger when he replied. "Not yet." He picked up the paper and placed it inside the green folder. "There are things I still need to show you and ask you first." Zalman sucked his teeth but said nothing.

The brown leather slid easily out of the envelope into his awaiting hand. Already so tattered, Jake had hesitated to look at the journal jacket too often after finding it. Instead, he let it rest inside the envelope where he had found it until now. Now, he let his hands read the skin, moving over smooth soft leather, turning it over in his palm until the horse, embossed on the outside of the jacket, faced him. "Do you know what this is?"

Zalman took the journal from him, "Of course. This was always with him. It started to come apart." Opening the book, his fingers plucked at the crumbled binding. "Pages from this are scattered across Europe. He wrote all the time in it. Your grandmother's map he tucked in here, helped us find our way out of Poland." He traced the Yiddish inscription, Isaac's proper name. "She had drawn him a map so he would know always where he was and where he was going." Zalman rubbed the leather in his hands. "He kept it here." The old man let his forehead rest in the soft cotton of his sleeve, not wanting this wet emotion, a wayward drop, to stain Ike's journal.

It hadn't occurred to Jake, it wouldn't have, that this one relic, a prized possession, might in some way belong to Zalman, too. A shudder curled the old man's spine in his chair and he tucked his head to the side, wiping eyelids across his sleeve. Still he held the journal in the palm of one hand, and with the other, he patted the cover gently.

When he lifted his head, his profile facing Jake, something inside of Zalman had settled. "I missed this. It is good to see again." He smiled at Jake, the creased skin under his eyes still dewy. "Thank you for showing me."

<hr>

She was finished setting the table and wondered if Jake couldn't arrange the Passover plate.

"I'm not sure how."

Erika motioned for him to follow her into the kitchen. On the counter by the window was laid out everything he would need: a lamb shank, boiled egg, mint, matzoh, a small bowl of haroset, and thin white slices of raw horseradish. "Follow the pictures, Jacob." She gestured to a gold platter with carved figures and Hebrew letters marking each item's placement. Jake opened the box of matzoh and carefully found and removed three perfect pieces, not cracked or crumbled in the corners, and set them down on the plate.

———

His mother, Rose, loved the holidays - all of them equally, the pleasant ones and the sad ones, too. Every year she would make the seder special just for the three of them. It was a good thing, this pleasure, these rituals which still belonged to her. She would light the candles in the kitchen with Jake at her side. Then they would sit at the table in the dining room using the fine dishes, bought as a present to herself with the money the government gave her. Her reparation china.

Ike would read through the Hagaddah, careful for Rose's sake not to miss a single word. The black letters of the book were Hebrew and the red letters were Yiddish. Jake would follow along in the paper book they had given him at Hebrew school, full of English translations and bright coloured illustrations.

When the spring came following her death, neither Jake nor Ike mentioned Passover, but one day, when Jake came home from school he found a sheet in the kitchen cupboard covering all of the bread, and boxes of matzoh on the counter. He asked his father if he should get dressed for the seder. "Who is going to cook a seder meal, you?" Ike peered at his son over the rim of his glasses. "Besides, it is just us two." Jake insisted they had to do something—it was almost sundown. What about the Hillel sandwiches, matzah with *maror* and *haroset*. "There is horseradish in the fridge. Eat what you want." Jake asked his father about the *haroset*, "We need both for the sandwich. Maror for the slaves' bitter tears and haroset for the mortar of the bricks the slaves used for the pyramids." Ike folded closed his newspaper. "Just remember the tears twice instead."

For the rest of the night, Jake stayed hidden inside his room. As his bedtime approached, a knock fell upon his door. Ike told him that there was half a loaf of bread still in the cupboard so he could make a sandwich to take to school. Already dressed in his pyjamas, Jake opened his door and stared up in his father's face, his cheeks raw, salt stained dry. "I can't eat bread. We never eat bread during Passover. Mom made me leftovers to take to school." He gasped when he spoke, out of breath, snot dried on his upper lip. Ike turned away, spoke to the doorframe rather than his son. "This is your mother's house. We will keep Passover in here. That is enough." He had already turned to walk away when Jake slammed the door.

He had not known it was there until it began to hurt less, not wholly felt it until it had already begun to heal. Seda had told him once that to get to know his father, he would first have to forgive him. It had all already begun to fall away when Jake decided to try.

"I think I understand him better now. You're not supposed to outlive everyone you love. My father did it twice."

"Almost," Zalman corrected. "Almost everyone. I think Izzy was so afraid of losing you... he couldn't bear it. It never occurred to him that you could lose him first. That he could make it happen. That he could disappear. Again. And yet, that is what he did."

The seder began at the first hint of sundown. The kitchen table, beautifully set with cotton napkins and two wine glasses each, sat near the patio doors, cracked open to let both a breeze and Eliyahu pass through. The table was round, no head, no foot. Erika rose from her seat across from Jake and, with the deft stroke of a wood match, lit the Passover candles, circling her hands over the budding flames. She covered her eyes and prayed by heart. Zalman thanked his wife and she returned to her seat at his side. Flipping through the pages of the Hagaddah, finding his place, ready to lead this little family through the recounting and retelling which holds up that night as different from every other night. He raised the first cup of syrupy dark wine in his left hand and read: *"Kos Kiddush,* the first cup, the cup of sanctification. Our story tells that in diverse ways, with different words, God gave to each of us a singular promise of freedom."

"Next we move to the *Yahatz*, a bond formed by sharing. I break the middle matzah and conceal one half as the *afikomen*. Later we will share it, as in days of old. Among people everywhere, sharing of bread, of the Passover meal and story, forms a bond of fellowship."

The Casablanca sun continued in its curving gesture across the skyline, ducking behind and between the buildings that lined the Weisses' street. Jake savoured the blend of green mint and salt as he ground the *karpas* between his teeth.

"*Koreh,* continuity with past tradition. Preserving a bond with the observance of our ancestors, we follow a practice of Hillel, from the time when the Temple stood. We do as he did so that we might preserve the precept handed down to him, as a son from his father."

Zalman spread the pages of the Hagaddah wide before him. Jake must remember; the reading would have been his as child. And so, as he was the youngest then, he was again. Jake read aloud the Four Questions, and, as he did, he felt the squeeze of Erika's hand reaching out to him across the ivory silk tablecloth.

"*Arba'at haminim,* the four sons. Four times the Torah bids us to tell our children of the Exodus. Four times the Torah repeats: 'And you shall tell your child on that day...' There are four sons: one wise, one wicked, one simple, and one that does not even know how to ask.

209

"It is the wise who want to know. And you shall tell him it is what the Lord did for *us* when we went forth..."

As Zalman continued the readings, his wife got up noiselessly out of her seat. Smells from the kitchen rose up, drifted around the men as they turned the page and began *Maggid*, the narration.

"Not only our ancestors alone did the Holy One redeem, but us as well, along with them as it is written. Therefore, even if all of us were wise, all of us people of understanding, all of us learned in Torah, it would still be our obligation to tell the story...

"And with this telling, all the firstborn males among your children shall you redeem."

Erika returned with soup bowls in hand. The Haggadot were cleared from the table, put aside where they could be reached later. Standing up from his seat, Zalman went to the sink to rinse his hands clean before the meal. With a single word, "Come," the old man invited Jake to do the same.

The morning after the seder, they had several hours before they would have to leave for the airport. Erika was on the phone with her sister, promising they would not be too late for dinner and reminding her to set the table for two extra, as they were bringing her nephew, Jacob, and her niece, Seda. Jake and Zalman were again seated in the living room, everything untouched and laid out as it had been the day before. Zalman leaned sideways in his chair, his elbow propped on a cushion and fingers laced, resting on his chest. Jake picked up the green folder and removed the two papers he had not wanted to discuss earlier. "There is something I want to do but I have some questions I need answered first. By you."

"Whatever I have is yours."

"About my father."

"Yours."

The corners of the page in front him curled and uncurled, rolled by his nervous fingers. "First, I need to know," a deep breath, the first of many, "did my father want me to find all of this?"

Zalman tilted his head, the skin between his eyes squeezed, unsure of the question.

"It was in his will that everything he had, everything in the house, was meant for me. That's what it said," Jake remembered the way the wording had surprised him. "It was 'meant' for me. This folder, all of this stuff, was right there in the middle of it."

Ten fingers rose and fell, a wave splashing on his chest. "I never knew Izzy to be careless, especially with his papers or his words. What do you think?"

"I think he wouldn't have expected me to bother to read any of it. Just throw the lot of it out. That's what I expected at least."

"You have too little faith for yourself."

"I mean, I did all of this running around and I need to know if I really did it all just for me."

Zalman simply shrugged. "It matters only what you think. After all the running, what did you learn?"

For the past several months, Jake had wondered himself what the answer to that question might be, the uncertainty of it always churning in the background of his thoughts. "I want to think that it was the best he could have left me, better than leaving me with nothing at all." Rotating it first so that the printed words would stand upright before Zalman, Jake turned over the white page in front of him and offered it across the table. "It's from the museum."

Zalman leaned forward and picked the top paper up with one hand, bringing it close in front of his face, blocking Jake from view. "The woman from the memorial museum who asked if I would write down my father's story. It's a form she gave me, with all the other papers." Jake reached into his folder and pulled out another page, this one folded in three so that all that could be seen was the Memorial Museum's letterhead. Jake unfolded the paper and handed it to Zalman. "It matches this one I found in his things. But he never filled it out, not the date or any of the information. Just his name and his birthday."

The handwriting on the two papers, so different, stretched across the lines on the identical forms: Name of survivor, _Yitzhak Andor Langlebben (Langley)_, Birth Date, _March 25, 1924_. Jake had copied his father's entry.

The air from Zalman's mouth tickled the paper before him, "So you are doing the right thing then?"

Jake sighed, shaking his head, "Well, I'm not sure if it's right or wrong."

Tipping the page, his wrist bent, Zalman looked at Jake. "The right thing."

"I need your help to do it." The tone of his voice lowered, as did his gaze, falling to focus somewhere on the table between them. "All of the running around, the research and the conversations. I learned about everyone else's story and what happened to them, But every time I looked for him in what they said, what he did or why, there was just... he still wasn't really there. I don't know enough of the details, the facts to tell his story."

Jake was still, unmoving he waited for Zalman's answer. Then a hand, Zalman's hand, slid over the tabletop into Jake's view, calling his eyes upward.

"We tell the stories that are ours to tell. He left it to you. It is your story now."

Jake told the old man that he didn't know where or how to begin. What line could Jake draw to say *yes, yes this is how it started*. But then, it began with a crash, didn't it, and the sound of stained glass blown into the streets. And what follows.

"The papers — the ones that they were saving?"

Zalman pinched his eyes tight, remembering. "Mmm. *Hashemot*. The names. The name of God."

"Yes, but also — I looked into it — records from the communities. Marriage records. Birth records."

"*Yo*, yes, those names too."

A knot thumped like a fist at the back of Jake's neck. "You said they had to burn some; others were just buried. And then with this, with his papers, it's like he turned his own basement into one of those graves."

"A grave or a *genizah*. Not much difference maybe."

"Why did he run? Why didn't he finish in Poland with his uncle and stay?"

"We ran together. I never thought we wouldn't be back. He always knew . . ." Zalman's eyes closed, squinting, making creases in the thin skin surrounding his lashes. "My father told me to go. I asked Izzy to come with me."

Opening his eyes, Jake could see fresh tears clinging to the old man's lashes. "I'm..." His voice caught in his throat, "I'm sorry".

"You saved his life." Jake felt wetness beginning to gather in the creases of his own eyes.

"I made him choose one life over another," Zalman sniffed loudly and shook his head.

Jake thought of the way Zalman had insisted on sitting with him at the shivah. The way he, too, had only one person for whom he could ever properly mourn. "I will tell you. I will tell you all of it. But first, do you know how your last name, your real name, Langlebben, comes from?"

At Jake's reply, Zalman clenched and unclenched his fist on the tabletop. "Izzy spoke of it over and over. After all, it is important to know from where you came. We start with that."

"Mazel Tov on your coming simcha! I was so glad to hear. Your father says to me how hard you are working. Your torah portion is not easy but it is one of the most important."

Thirteen-year-old Jake stared at his father's slippered feet, the toes just visible in the doorway from where Ike stood, and listened, just around the corner. He wasn't sure whose idea it had been, just that he was dragged down from his room so that his "uncle" could congratulate him and discuss his bar mitzvah torah portion over the phone. "He says you are find-ing problems."

Jake knew from the sound on the other end, wet suction, that it was his turn to speak. "No. No one wants to hear what I want to write." A slight shuffle of the disembodied feet warned Jake to watch his tone. "It just bothers me. His dad has just tied him up and tried to kill him." A puff of air escaped the plastic padding as Jake dropped himself into a kitchen chair.

"But he hears again the voice of God and stops."

"Yeah but," Jake gently kicked the nearest table leg. "He starts for no reason then he stops for no reason. And Isaac isn't even mad." He cannot hear it, but Zalman smiled into the phone. "He doesn't say anything, neither of them do. They just go off together like nothing happened."

"It is a passage about faith, Jacob. Abraham must prove his faith in God when he is asked for sacrifice without reason. And he must have faith again when he is asked without reason to stop. And for the son, he must have faith in the father."

Jake's foot rocked the table with a final, conclusive *thud*.

"It doesn't make sense. Why should he trust his father ever again? Or God? The kid almost dies and that's it, they don't even bother saying how he feels. "

"Very true. But then no one says how Abraham feels, either."

The kitchen was dim with all the lights off, though the sun still hung in the air outside. *Indian summer*, Ike thought, practicing the term he had heard on the news.

Ike had waited to hear Jake's bedroom door shut before returning to his conversation with his friend.

"You could have spoken with him for yourself," said Zalman. "You are more versed than I."

"I don't know how to talk to him anymore. And I don't know how to talk about those things anymore either." Scripture. Faith. Fatherhood. Ike slipped a foot out of his slipper and let the ball of his bare foot be cooled by the linoleum floor. "I thought it would sound better coming from you."

"Not true," Zalman's deep bray of a laugh momentarily filled up the phone line. "He is smart to ask questions. You should be smart enough to answer them."

"Zeama... not now. It's late and I'm tired."

Zalman paid his old friend's interjection no mind. "It is different for him than it is for you." It is the difference of being able to see the faces of a past which haunts you and being blind but haunted all the same.

Later that night, as he turned off the lights throughout the house, Ike thought about when he told him. Had told his son that Rojina was dead. Not sleeping, not sick or in one of her moods. Just gone. Jake had refused to believe it. He was so serious, so sure. "No," he said. "She's not gone. She goes away but she always comes back. She goes to her room for a few days but then she comes out and she hugs me and says, 'I'm sorry. Mommy was just a little sad.' And then, she's back." It was then the boy had started blinking back tears, "Moms don't go away."

It was a childish thing to say. Ike could see in his son's face that he knew it too, something a child much younger would say, but they both wanted so badly for it to be true.

Ike couldn't help it. He knew what he was about to say was wrong, knew even then that he would regret it for the rest of his life. (And he did.) But he said it, because it was true. And because he was hurting too. "Moms go away. Everyone goes away."

Midday heat glazed the black-grey concrete stretched for miles beyond the airport window. A tide of cool air made its way up from the vents that ran along the window, tickling Jake's chin as he rested his forehead against the glass. Seda's airplane finished snaking its way down the asphalt alley towards the gate. He could see the men in their nylon vests pushing out the metal stairs to meet the plane, propeller wind rippling their clothing. Jake stood upright, lifting his head away, the imprint of his skin left lingering on the glass, and went to join Zalman and Erika standing by the escalator.

"She's here. We should go down to the gate now."

Standing on the grated step, Erika twisted her body to look up at Jake on the stair above her. Balancing on the shiny black railing, Jake leaned far forward, his neck bent, searching the crowd. "Don't worry." She smiled up into his face, her cheek dipping to one side, "People always find each other. One way," and then back again, "or another."

As they descended into the departure level, a cluster of other families and friends crowded the floor in front of the gate. The automatic doors had already parted and Jake skimmed the assembly for her familiar face, her walk as she would make her way through the pile-up of strangers. With Zalman and Erika standing off to the side, he waded his way into the crowd, craning his neck to look through the open arrival doors onto the tarmac. From behind him, he heard Zalman laugh, a big laugh, reverberating in his heavy bouncing chest. Jake turned, his eyes and ears tuned to the sound. She had found them, hovering at the rim of the crowd. Seda was wrapped up in Erika's embrace, her head perched on the older woman's shoulder as she bent her knees to match Erika's height. Jake began to make his way back to them. Seda looked up and met his eyes.

יאָרצײַט
ANNIVERSARY

Jake hadn't been back since the unveiling. And even then, he hadn't been able to bring himself to stand in front of his father's new tombstone, the words so recently carved into granite. He had chosen a black tone of stone because he thought Ike would find it appropriately somber. Other than that, Jake had ensured in every other way that it matched his mother's, with the Star of David in the top left corner and the menorah in the top right. That is where he had stood almost a year ago now, on his way home from the Holocaust Centre, his hands stuffed into pockets, one of which was full of paper. Jake hadn't told anyone it was the unveiling, not Seda or Leah, even though he knew how much each would have wanted to come; instead, he came alone and stood for some time at Rose's graveside. He had always been closer to her, and it still felt somehow strange and too fresh to think of his father there with her.

Now, a year later, he stands between his parents and reaches into the backpack he's brought with him.

There are no flowers here, not by any of the memorials laid out row by row in the heart of the city. Instead, there are stones. They sit on top or in front of the headstones, little communities of rock, piled on top of each other. Some believe that

221

the stones weigh down the soul to keep the dead with us. Others accept that the dead are gone, but the stones — with their weight and permanence — symbolize memory. A physical reminder of whom and what has been lost—one that can't wilt or fade with time. Unmoving. Solid.

Brushing off the top of his mother's tombstone, Jake places three rocks; one each for him and Seda, and one for Zalman, selected personally from his own garden at the end of their last visit. It is unlike the others, a decorative garden rock, white and rough with flecks of silver that pick up the light bouncing on the snow all around him.

Zalman has sent Jake with a stone for Ike, as well. This one deep blue and polished, marbled throughout with streaks of teal and turquoise, baby blue and grey. It is a memory unto itself, of a gate and a new start and Zalman wanted Ike to have it. To look down and know that he is remembered. Jake bends down and puts the beautiful blue rock in the snow just in front of his father's tombstone and, reaching back into his bag, pulls out four more. One for him, one for Seda. One for Mina, and one for Chaim.

Standing up, he thinks for a moment about trying to remember the mourner's kaddish, to pay his proper respects the way his great uncle would. Instead, he decides to tell his parents a story. It begins with a crash in the night.

EPILOGUE

Tamuz 5713

July 1950

Everyone here is too close. I can feel the breath of what feels like hundreds of strangers on my neck and cheeks. Their faces are hopeful, but I see the fear in their eyes, the worry. It is familiar and it is right.

The boat pitches to the right, and the young girl beside me grabs my arm. It is an instinct keeping her from falling but her hand lingers even after the boat steadies. I stood in front of her as we were boarding, and she has been within an arm's distance of me ever since. She is travelling alone and so am I. Unspoken, we have decided to be each other's family for now. Someone to keep warm beside at night, to make small talk as the day drags on, to reach out to when you lose your balance which it seems she does a lot. It wasn't until the second day she told me her name, Margalit. I wrote it in my journal in both Hebrew and English to show her, trying to teach her as many words as I can before we dock, and our temporary family becomes just two orphans once again.

Another rock and my stomach turns over. I bend down and press my forehead against the cool railing, holding on tightly with my left hand to keep myself steady. Without thinking about it, my right hand rises to the side of my face, searching for *pais* my heart knows are no longer there. A childish habit, wrapping my fingers in the curls, like sucking my thumb, and one I must break. There is nothing there now, no markers on me anywhere. The few times I have had a chance to look in a mirror recently, I hardly recognize myself. The face in the mirror is not the same, this change cannot be undone. But it is better that way.

Margalit pulls on my coat, she needs to sit again. Still holding on to the cold metal above, I sink against the wall beside her and watch in awe as within minutes, she is fast asleep. She mumbles under her breath, talking in her dreams. Whispering to her mother. I try to let myself do the same, try to let myself sleep, hoping I too can visit my mother, let this boat rock me to sleep and bring me to her. Just in case, I say her name and my father's quietly to myself, asking them to come to me, come with me, waiting, waiting for sleep.

GLOSSARY OF YIDDISH, HEBREW, AND POLISH TERMS

CHAPTER ONE – בְּכוֹר

זָכוֹר – (zākhor) Hebrew term basically meaning to remember, to record, or to reinvent.

בְּכוֹר – (bi-khor) Hebrew term used to refer to the eldest son.

SHIVAH – Hebrew, meaning 'seven', refers to the week of mourning after a Jewish funeral. The family of the deceased receives visitors at the family home for seven days. Immediate family members traditionally sit in low, hard chairs for the shivah week as well as observing other outward practices of mourning, including wearing ripped clothing.

SHTETL – Primarily Jewish towns and villages in Eastern Europe.

WORT – Yiddish, 'Word'

CHAPTER TWO – כִּסְלֵו

כִּסְלֵו – (key-slev) Kislev is the third month of the Hebrew calendar.

ABBA – Hebrew, 'Father'

BETH MIDRASH – Religious school for higher learning, older boys.

CHAI – (high) The letters correspond to the number 18, meaning 'life.' Multiples of 18 may be referred to as *chai*.

CHEDER – Religious school for young boys.

DAVEN – Hebrew, 'To pray'

EREV SHABBAS – The night that is the beginning of the Sabbath, Friday night.

GENIZAH – Hebrew, literally meaning 'hiding place.' A storeroom or cabinet for worn-out sacred writings called *shemot* because they contained God's name or reference to God. Every synagogue will have a genizah. Cemeteries and religious community centers may also have a genizah.

GENIZOT – plural of Genizah

HAMOR – Hebrew, 'Donkey'

HAZAR – Yiddish, 'Pig'

KIPPAH – Head covering for Jewish males.

NEEMAN – Head of the Jewish community.

PAIS – Sideburns found on religious Jewish males.

SCHVITZ – Yiddish, 'Sweat'

SHABBAS – the Sabbath

SHEMOT – Hebrew, 'Names'. Also refers to the papers stored in a genizah which contain the name of God.

SHOLEM-ALEYCHEM – Yiddish greeting

SHTIEBL – Prayer houses, more casual and smaller than synagogues.

SHULHOYF – Synagogue courtyard, often the center of the shtetl.

YESHIVAH – Traditional religious school.

CHAPTER THREE - הַ נָ מֵ ר וְהַ קַ צָב

הַנָמֵר וְהַשׁוֹחֵט – (ha-na-mār veh-ha-sho-ket) The tiger and the butcher.

AROP – Yiddish, 'Down'

CZERWIEC – Polish, month of June. Literally meaning 'Worms'.

CHEVRA KADISHa – Burial society who oversee preparation of bodies and burial according to Jewish law.

ESN – Yiddish, 'Eat'

GUT – Yiddish, 'Good'

KLUGER – Yiddish, A smart person

LISTOPAD - Polish, month of November. Literally meaning 'Falling leaves.'

NUDNIK – Yiddish, A pest or a bore

SHOCHET – Ritual slaughterer (or person in charge of overseeing ritual slaughter) of meat and poultry in accordance with Jewish kosher laws.

STYCZEN – Polish, month of January. Literally meaning 'Rod' or 'Pole.'

CHAPTER FOUR - קלוגה קינדער

קלוגה קינדער – (kluge kinder) Wise children

BOYCHIK – Yiddish, Affectionate term for a young boy.

LIB – Yiddish, 'Dear'

MEZUZOT – The plural of mezuzah, parchment scroll with selected Torah passages in small container attached to doorframes.

CHAPTER FIVE - פִּידְיוֹן הַבֵּן

פִּידְיוֹן הַבֵּן – (pidyon ha-ben) Redemption of the First Born

AFIKOMEN – The middle piece of matzah on the Passover plate.

HAGADDAH – Meaning 'telling', it is the book that contains the order of the Passover seder.

HAROSET – Sweet mixture of nuts and fruits representing mortar in the Passover story.

KARPAS – Refers to green vegetable used in Passover seder.

ACKNOWLEDGEMENTS

This book has been a long time in the making and would not have come to fruition if not for the guidance and support of several people. I want to thank my early readers, including Jennifer Andrews, Sarah Neville and Liat Kirmayer, and my later readers, including Megan Lamb and Teresa Wong, who gave not only her time, encouragement and guidance but words for this cover, as well. In that vein, my thanks to Naomi Lewis whose support has meant so much, and Rabbi Mark Glickman, who ensured my religious references were on point.

Interviews conducted before writing began gave me the confidence to assume the voice of a young man in a world so far from my own. To Aron Eichler, a special thanks more than I was ever able to say. To Rabbi M. Matusof for picking up where his wife left off and to Freda Plucer for always telling her story, thank you.

Over two decades ago, something wonderful happened and a serendipitous meeting brought two wonderful men into my life: Alberto Manguel and Craig Stephenson. I told them I wanted to be a writer and right away, though I had not proven myself to them in any way, they both believed in me and treated me as if I already was one. Thank you for that and for being believers in this story.

I would like to thank my mother, Willa, who was willing to get so invested in the writing process that she actually fought with me over what fictional characters would think and do. And my father, Malcolm, for repeatedly answering questions like: "Okay, it's 1974 and I'm going out for dinner. Where am I going and what am I wearing?" Thank you to Jessica and Jon for being beside me every day. You have all been more support than you know. And to my husband, Tony, and my children, thank you. You are the best part of my story.

Lastly, I would like to acknowledge and express my deep gratitude to everyone who lent me their name – first, middle, or last.

Made in United States
Orlando, FL
08 July 2025

62739138R00134